MÉLANIE MORAND

DONALD ANTRIM is the author of the novels *Elect Mr. Robinson for a Better World*, *The Hundred Brothers* (both published by Granta) and *The Verificationist*, as well as the memoir *The Afterlife*. Antrim has received grants and awards from the John D. and Catherine T. MacArthur Foundation, the John Simon Guggenheim Memorial Foundation and the National Endowment for the Arts. He is a frequent contributor to the *New Yorker* and teaches in the MFA program at Columbia University.

ALSO BY DONALD ANTRIM

FICTION

Elect Mr. Robinson for a Better World
The Hundred Brothers
The Verificationist

NONFICTION

The Afterlife: A Memoir

ADDITIONAL PRAISE FOR
THE EMERALD LIGHT IN THE AIR

'Graceful and finely-crafted ... A strain of surreal and tender humour is never far from the surface. The success of the writing lies in its tone – the narrative voice is funny and sad, elegant and offbeat, brutal and merciful, careful and mysterious. Tension builds with slow precision right until the strange often unexpected conclusions' *Irish Times*

'Donald Antrim [is] one of the sharpest, funniest, darkest writers of his generation. Mr. Antrim produces so little that every book is an event, and, like everything else he has done, this one is a careful treasure' Bill Buford, *Wall St Journal*

'*The Emerald Light in the Air* spans 16 years, and across its seven stories a trajectory of style and theme – a turn from the comic exaggeration and cultural and historical saturation of the three novels toward a pressurised, often grave psychological realism. [Antrim] a disciple of Barthelme conquers the territory of Cheever and Updike – [the result] is stunning' Christian Lorentzen, *London Review of Books*

THE

EMERALD LIGHT

IN THE AIR

THE
EMERALD LIGHT
IN THE AIR

Stories

DONALD ANTRIM

GRANTA

Granta Publications, 12 Addison Avenue, London W11 4QR

First published in Great Britain by Granta Books, 2014
This paperback edition published by Granta Books, 2015
First published in the United States by Farrar, Straus and Giroux, New York, in 2014
Copyright © 2014 by Donald Antrim

The right of Donald Antrim to be identified as the author
of this work has been asserted by him in accordance
with the Copyright, Designs and Patents Act, 1988.

The stories in this collection were originally published,
in slightly different form, in the *New Yorker*.

A CIP catalogue record for this book
is available from the British Library.

1 3 5 7 9 10 8 6 4 2

ISBN 978 1 84708 651 8
eISBN 978 1 84708 650 1

Designed by Jonathan D. Lippincott

Offset by M Rules

Printed and bound by CPI Group (UK) Ltd, Croydon, CR0 4YY

www.grantabooks.com

MIX
Paper from
responsible sources
FSC® C020471

for Deborah Treisman

CONTENTS

THE

EMERALD LIGHT

IN THE AIR

AN ACTOR PREPARES

Lee Strasberg, a founder of the Group Theatre and the great teacher of the American Method, famously advised his students never to "use"—for generating tears, etc., in a dramatic scene—personal/historical material less than seven years in the personal/historical past; otherwise, the Emotion Memory (the death of a loved one or some like event in the actor's life that can, when evoked through recall and substitution, hurl open the floodgates, as they say, right on cue, night after night, even during a long run)—this material, being *too close*, as it were, might overwhelm the artist and compromise the total control required to act the part or, more to the point, act it well; might, in fact, destabilize the play; if, for instance, at the moment in a scene when it becomes necessary for Nina or Gertrude or Macduff to wipe away tears and get on with life; if, at that moment, it becomes impossible for a wailing performer to pull it together; if, in other words, the *performer* remains trapped in affect long after the *character* has moved on to dinner or the battlefield—when this happens, then you can be sure that delirious theatrical mayhem will follow.

What is the point in all this? Strasberg was wrong. Seven years are not enough, a fact I discovered recently during a twilight performance of *A Midsummer Night's Dream*, presented on the college green to commemorate the founding, a hundred and fifty years ago, by the Reverend William Trevor Barry— my great-great-grandfather on my father's side—of the small liberal-arts institution that bears our family's name and our seal. I am Reginald Barry, Dean of Student Life and Wm. T. Barry Professor of Speech and Drama at Barry College, so naturally it fell to me to direct our commemorative, barefoot production of Shakespeare's great festive comedy. While I was at it, I decided to serve up some ham myself, as Lysander. What would a skinny, balding, unmarried, childless forty-six-year-old Lysander—a PhD with hair on his back—*mean* within the context of an otherwise college-age show? I'm not sure I can answer that question. Normally, Lysander would be essayed by some good-looking lacrosse goalie waiting his turn to date-rape the beautiful, waifish Mary Victoria Frost, our Hermia, only a sophomore herself and already the finest actress we've had in my time at Barry, a sure candidate for Yale, or Juilliard if she can ease off the drugs. I might stand in as Egeus or Theseus, or maybe Oberon, King of the Faeries, if I felt up to it. But high-concept casting is a director's prerogative. Two seasons ago, we mounted an all-male, all-nude *Taming of the Shrew*. People said it increased their appreciation for the radical potentials in Elizabethan drama.

And so, the play. Four adolescents turned out by law and their parents into a green world governed by spooks, all playing—children and their phantoms—at love and nighttime evil.

The adolescents were me, Mary Victoria Frost, Sheila Tannenbaum, as Helena, and Billy Valentine, as Demetrius. Sheila, a junior, plays character parts when she's not playing basketball for the Lady Bears, and I knew she'd make an acceptable if not entirely agreeable Helena, with her big hands and lurching walk and brown eyes too far apart on an otherwise bent-looking, asymmetrical face; but Valentine represented a casting risk. Valentine is a certain kind of blond-haired, upper-middle-class boy—the type is familiar at any private school in the land, I would imagine—a sarcastic, wiry little underachiever who, on the basis of no evidence, is rumored among his peers to be a genius.

"Don't come to rehearsals stoned, Billy," I warned this kid before first read-through.

"*Stoned*, Mr. Barry?" He laughed. The previous Friday, a bunch of us had found ourselves lying around on sofas in my office in Lower Hancock, getting wasted on some of Billy's very strong homegrown.

"We're here to work," I told him now, and he said, "Don't you think I should be playing Puck?"

"You want to direct this show, Valentine?" I asked him. "No? Then let me worry about casting."

"Hey, Mr. Barry. Everything's cool. It's just that Martin can't read his script. I mean, he can't *see*."

Billy Valentine had a point. Putting Martin Epps in as Puck was like putting, well, I don't know what into what. How can you defend a totally blind Robin Goodfellow tapping his way around the stage with a telescoping cane, except in theory?

Dramaturgically speaking, the theory was sound enough, I thought; and so I opened up rehearsals by reciting it—in somewhat oblique form—to my cast. There they were, the "drama mafia," down in the windowless Hancock Hall basement, twenty-five or thirty hungover Lovers, Royals, Spirit Wraiths, Merry Men, stagehands, set techies, and walk-ons, all dressed in late-spring cutoffs and oxford-cloth shirts and sheer halter tops, almost every one of this lot—except Martin Epps, the blind boy—inhaling drags off cigarettes; it was a bored, blasé-looking crowd. "Genuine vision, expressed artistically by Shakespeare in the character Puck, is more than the ability to open your eyes, take a look around, and see what's wrong with your life," I announced to these oversexed dope addicts.

No one spoke or even looked up, and I had that terrible feeling I get at the kickoff to any rehearsal period, when I realize how much disappointment lies ahead. I said, "Well, anyway, Theseus, it's your line to start the play."

Still no one spoke. "Danielle, do you have the cast list?" I asked my sophomore stage manager.

"Hang on, Mr. Barry, it's here somewhere."

"Call me Reg," I told her. "During the play, we're all equals."

She stared at me like she wasn't quite sure. Unorthodox etiquette is often perplexing for the young. She held up the cast list and waved it—apparently some kind of "theatrical" gesture—in the air over her head. "Greg Lippincott, you're Theseus."

"Oh, is that how 'Theseus' is pronounced?" Greg asked. It was hard to believe he was one of the Philadelphia Lippincotts. He took a puff from his cigarette. Snickering could be heard. It took four hours to complete the read-through. Danielle delivered Martin Epps's lines to him, and Martin repeated each back, painstakingly, one word then the next, like a spy being briefed on a plan.

"I'll put a girdle round about the earth in forty minutes," recited Danielle.

"I'll. Put. A girdle. Round about the earth. In forty minutes," said Martin.

I made a note to ask him to pick up the pace and not tap cadences on the floor with his cane. I made another note, to Jim Ferguson, warning him to avoid inserting "like" into Oberon's speeches to Titania. I worried about telling the faeries and goblins that their costumes would consist of G-strings and pasties.

I can always give thanks, in these delicate situations, for our costumer, my girlfriend, Carol.

Carol came in later in the week, during our first walk-through rehearsal, and made the case for her skimpy outfits.

"I think we will be able to see from their attire that these faeries are playful and very dangerous, earthy yet devilish, with a heightened insistence on gender that not only subverts our own male-dominated culture but underscores the young lovers' cruelty toward one another in the Athenian grove," she announced while staring straight at me. Was it necessary for Carol to see *everything* as a reflection of the sexual antagonisms in our on-again, off-again relationship?

She held the faerie sketches—Cobweb, Peaseblossom, Moth, and Mustardseed—up in glaring overhead light. A girl wearing shorts and a T-shirt objected: "No way. I'm not going out there naked."

"This is the theater, honey. The character is naked, not you."

"Good point, Carol," I interjected, unwisely. Carol gave me one of her furious looks, reminding me that she was approaching a breaking point in our love affair. What can be said about this? After five years, it's a regular enough occurrence. The truth is that we've never been very happy together. We pick at each other and have squalid fights. I'll spare the details, except to say that whenever I think about our fighting, or about Carol's drinking, I feel sad for us both; and this makes me want to phone her up and find out if she's doing all right; and *this* behavior, as will easily be understood by anyone who has lasted even a short while in a hostile erotic relationship, is almost invariably a prelude to knockout sex.

"What will *I* be wearing" called a boy from the back of the basement. The boy was Sam English, a theater regular, bearded and deep-voiced; he was my Bottom. Carol said to him and to the entire cast, "Costumes are designed to suggest historical period and class, while also referring to modern dress. Bottom and his fellow Mechanicals will wear weight-lifting belts over wool tunics with the characters' names ironed on."

It had been my idea to depict Shakespeare's vulgar trades-men as a team of Elizabethan power lifters. I imagined them carrying six-packs of beer hanging from clear plastic rings. "Let me see Bottom and his men at the front of the room, pronto," I called out, to begin that day's walk-through of the play within the play, act five's irresistible "tedious brief scene of young Pyramus and his love Thisbe."

Here came Quince, the carpenter; Bottom, the weaver; Flute, the bellows-mender; Snout, the tinker; Snug, the joiner; and Starveling, the tailor—in reality a cluster of political-science and religious-studies majors. These six huddled around me, and I said, "You guys are fuckups and you're ugly. You're a bunch of functionally illiterate dipsomaniacs, and I'd be amazed if any of you has ever been laid. Your own mothers ought to be ashamed of you."

The boys looked confused, and I knew I had them where I wanted them. It is useful, when directing, to blur the boundaries between actor and role, to inaugurate, with a few stringent words, if necessary, a certain emotional instability; in this instance I was exploiting my students' routine insecuri-ties in order to lead them to identify with Shakespeare's motley artisans.

I then gave these Merry Men my cautionary talk about the hardships of a life in the theater. At some point, I became aware of Danielle—I could see her over Sam English's big head; she was waving and pointing at her watch, making those gestures and absurd faces people make when they need your attention, yet are afraid of you—so I concluded, "Boys, the point is this. People think the theater is romantic and magical. And some-times it is. But most of the time it's just a pile of crap that nobody cares about."

"Time for animal improvisations!" Danielle shouted.

A Midsummer Night's Dream, historians tell us, was probably first presented at a royal wedding held in the summer at a house outside London. Presumably, the guests, like wedding guests throughout history, became intoxicated with alcohol and the aphrodisiacal spirit of the occasion. Young couples, wandering in and out of doors, slipping away to flirt or break up or make love, had dramatic counterparts in the unhappy children lost in love in Shakespeare's imaginary grove. How many real lovers woke after the ceremony, hungover and sick, to discover themselves entwined on the lawn with mates met only during the festivities the night before? I wanted to create a world where love is mercurial, unbridled, bestial. In our production of *A Midsummer Night's Dream*, the unmarried lovers would fall asleep after chasing one another through the forest; then, doused with nectar from Puck's flower, they would roll over, rub their eyes, and fuck the wrong person.

"Let's all get down on our hands and knees," I told the cast.

Down we went. Right away I noticed that Mary Victoria Frost and several faeries appeared to be acting like house cats; these girls arched their backs, projected feline butts into the air, and hissed. Sheila Tannenbaum—who, in act two, scene one, repeats the famous line "Use me but as your spaniel, spurn me, strike me"—was doing a nice job as a submissive pup, rolling over and sticking out her tongue to lick Billy Valentine, slithering past on his belly. Lion roared and Bottom brayed like an ass, and Sarah Goldwasser, our Titania, responded by rubbing herself against Sam; it was clear that these two had a flirtation in the works. That's something I like to see. Sex makes any show better. "Oink, oink," I said to Mary Victoria Frost.

I love the theater. I really do. And I adored my cast. They adored one another, too; these boys and girls were becoming—as the days became weeks and the play took its shape—uninhibitedly smitten with one another. It was mid-May, and summer's first warmth was in the air. The basement felt stuffy and hot, thanks to the overheating furnace in the corner.

"We're not out of the woods yet," I announced at the beginning of our third week. "Those of you who haven't got off book, you're holding the rest of us up. Demetrius, time your entrances so you don't keep Helena waiting downstage. Titania, less kissing and more teasing when you're giving it up to Bottom in act four. Make him work for it."

"Reg?" peeped a voice from the crowd. It was Sarah Gold-wasser, the prima donna.

"Yes, Sarah?"

"When will we get out of this gross basement and start rehearsing on the green?"

"Any day now. Roger and Emil are building the platforms in the trees, and they have to dig the hole for Puck. Once Puck's crater is finished, we'll move the show outdoors."

"Crater?" This from Martin Epps.

"That's right. In our *Midsummer Night's Dream*, the demons won't merely buzz around like woodland pixies; they'll come right up from the earth to grab us and pull us down to Hell. At any rate, Martin, I don't think your hole will be much of a problem after one or two on-site rehearsals. You'll see," I assured the blind boy.

It was one of those moments when a person (myself, in this instance) says something wholly untoward, and then, becoming aware of the faux pas and its implications, rushes blindly forward—there is no other way to describe this adequately, except as a king of verbal blindness—exclaiming additional horrors. "What I meant is . . . the rest of us will . . . watch you crawling . . . covered with dirt and sticks . . . You can picture it . . . I don't mean literally . . ."

"That's okay, Mr. Barry," said Martin Epps.

"Call me Reg," I reminded him, by way of apology. Then, addressing the room at large, attempting to regain authority:

"All right. Let me have all the young lovers over in the corner. Lovers, don't touch the boiler."

Possibly—I should say probably—it was risky of me to attempt simulated sex with undergraduates.

"What do you think, gang? Is this something you feel you can comfortably do in front of an audience?"

Together we sat—Mary Victoria Frost, Sheila Tannenbaum, Billy Valentine, and I—in a cozy circle on the floor. Billy, I noticed, had his eye on Mary; he leaned back beside her, and you could tell he was angling to spy an opening in her blouse and glimpse a breast. Mary spoke: "How dark will it be?"

"Fairly. By act three, the sun will be setting. With any luck, it'll be a humid night and the fireflies will be out."

"It's going to be beautiful!" exclaimed Sheila.

I concurred, "That's right, Sheila. When you make love, you're doing God's work on Earth."

After that, we sat for a time. The atmosphere became pleasantly uncomfortable. This sensation of a pervasive, shared emotional discomfort may have been helped along by the presence nearby of the foul-smelling oil furnace, hissing and burning, making the air in our little corner feel sickeningly, suffocatingly warm. Finally Billy broke the tension with a homophobic joke. "Reg, will I have to make out with you?"

"In a manner of speaking, Billy. Lysander, Hermia, Demetrius, and Helena will trade back and forth in a kind of blind, revolving embrace. Erotic possibility, signifying not immorality but immortality, is the real pleasure for unmarried lovers. So we're going to get it on."

"Like in my dormitory," laughed Valentine.

Later, we all stretched out on the floor and began mapping positions. It was clear that the kids were—how shall I put this?—experienced in some ways and inexperienced in others. Sheila Tannenbaum chuckled when touched; there was little that was pretty about this rangy girl, yet she was coy and therefore sexy. Billy Valentine was not sexy. It annoyed me to watch him grope Mary Victoria Frost. He had no moves, and she, as far as I could tell, didn't care. I signaled everyone to switch partners, and Mary wrapped her legs around me. I read this as permission to cradle her in my lap. She weighed practically nothing. Was she one of those girls who exist on breakfast cereal and amphetamines? I stuck my face in her hair and breathed in her smells of bath oil and nicotine. Oh, my heart. I laid my head on Mary's shoulder and watched Billy Valentine straddle Sheila. He appeared to be mauling the girl's throat—what was he doing, administering a "sleeper" hold?—until Sheila made an athletic move with her legs, scissoring Billy and bringing him hard to the floor. *Thump.* Quickly, I leaned over and tugged Sheila toward me, in this way getting two girls and scoring a sexual victory over a boy young enough to be my son.

Billy Valentine sat to the side with his legs crossed and his head down. I had the feeling, watching him, that I was seeing him in an unguarded moment, and in a posture and attitude that expressed an essential state of his being. I was witnessing, it occurred to me, something like pure sadness; and I would've bet money that Billy was the child of divorced, probably alcoholic parents. I cuddled the girls and, in a moment of, I suppose, empathy, told him, "You know, Billy, my mother and father got drunk and argued all the time. The truth is, they were terrible to each other. I thought I'd never get over all that, and I guess maybe I never have."

For an instant, Billy looked as if he might laugh. But he didn't laugh. He gazed at me with these big, round eyes that seemed to grow larger and more rounded; and his whole countenance changed, which is to say that, in some way that had more to do with a feeling than an actual look, his expression softened, and he lowered his head.

"Places for act two, scene one!" I called out to Danielle

and the cast. "We're going to run the play from Puck's line to the faerie, 'Thou speak'st aright; I am that merry wanderer of the night.' Puck, you're downstage left, crawling out of your hole."

"Thou speak'st aright. I am that merry. Wanderer of the night," intoned my sightless Puck.

"Wait a minute, Martin. Do the line again, this time as if you hate life. Say this line as if you're alone in the world and you despise yourself."

"Thou speak'st aright; I am that"—here he paused for an especially long time, as if thinking about a hard problem—"merry wanderer of the night."

"Listen to me. Puck is not some frolicking clown. He's Hobgoblin! Beelzebub! Lucifer! Satan, the enemy of love! Puck is a wretched, willfully destructive creature. Let's do a quick exercise. Repeat after me: I am a wretched, willfully destructive creature."

"I am a wretched, willfully destructive. Creature."

"Everything I do creates pain."

"Everything I. Do creates pain."

"No one loves me."

"No. One loves me."

"I'm fucked up."

"I'm fucked . . ."

He was sniffling. His voice cracked. Were there tears? I could not see the young actor's eyes because they were hidden behind dark lenses. I leaned close to my Puck, in order to growl in his ear, "I wear the number of the beast."

"Huh?" he whimpered.

I smacked the blind kid on the shoulder. "Let's run this play, Martin, I mean Puck. When we get to the section where you chase the young lovers through the forest, go ahead and swat our legs with your cane."

And to the cast, the Royals and rude Mechanicals, the

devils and imps and lost children, I proclaimed, "This show needs to *move*, people. It's a comedy!"

Or is it? Students of *A Midsummer Night's Dream* will undoubtedly be familiar with the trend, in recent years, to emphasize horror in the drama: faeries played as ghouls, Oberon as a molester; Bottom's transformation depicted as a grotesque, literally asinine mutilation. There is a reactionary aspect to this movement away from traditional fun and games; construing the *Dream* as a hellish sexual nightmare rather than as an innocuous garden party is a way of making the play interestingly "modern" in the post–world war, post-Holocaust, thermonuclear and psychoanalytic era.

"Make it ugly," I instructed my cast in the final week before the show. It was a Sunday afternoon, our first—and only, thanks to storms blowing in—outdoor run-through. The day was overcast and unseasonably chilly, with winds from the north smelling like rain. Crows perched on tree branches and the faeries' wooden platforms, three plywood decks connected by swaying footbridges, everything balanced precariously in the high, heavy oak limbs that reached out to shade Puck's deep hole, dug "center stage" at the southernmost edge of the Barry College green, our theater.

"Up in the trees, faeries, let's go," I called. Girls took turns climbing. A few had trouble getting up. Sarah Goldwasser, the regal Titania, marched over and said, "Reg, will you tell Oberon to stop grabbing my nipples in our fight scene?"

"I think it's kind of good for the scene, Sarah."

"He does it too hard. My nipples don't like it that hard," she said, and huffed off toward her bower.

"Here comes the rain," a boy's voice beside me exclaimed.

"I'd appreciate it if you would concentrate on your acting and not worry about the weather, Billy."

"How are we supposed to do any acting when the entire stage is nothing but a hole in the ground?"

The boy had a point. And I had an answer. "The circular patterns sketched by our movements around the pit will illustrate mankind's proximity to the abyss, and this in turn will be a dramaturgical reminder of the themes of revolution and renewal in English morris dancing, which, you'll recall from the first week of rehearsal, Billy, is an acknowledged folk source for Shakespeare's May Day comedies."

I wish I could say I was pleased with this impromptu oration. Purely technical observations concerning the larger implications of stagecraft are best left in the classroom, having, out here in the field, as it were, more of a confusing than a clarifying effect. Billy looked despairing. Clearly I had been right, during that sex-scene rehearsal the week before, in supposing him to be the child of an unhappy home. I put my hand on his shoulder and said, in as fatherly a voice as I could concoct on short notice, "I know it's a mighty big hole, Billy. We'll all have to be careful not to fall in and break our legs. Sometimes in the theater, as in life, we do our best work when mainly concerned with not making fools of ourselves."

"That's typical for a man to say, isn't it?" declared a woman's voice. I became immediately tense. The speaker was Carol, who had snuck up from behind and was standing with her arms crossed before her chest, the posture expressing her confrontational mode, surely an indication that she had been drinking.

"Hello, Carol."

"Don't bother being polite, Reg," Carol said. "It doesn't look good on you." She was weaving slightly, actually swaying in place, much in the manner of an actor impersonating a drunk, I thought. Here was an example of a dramatic cliché's analogue in reality.

"We're about to begin rehearsal, Carol. I suppose you've come to take a few last-minute costume measurements?"

"Fuck you."

"Let's not have one of our scenes, Carol, not out here in front of the boy, please?"

"Look who's talking. If it isn't the protector of youth himself." She addressed Billy, "I'll bet you're fond of your teacher, aren't you?"

"I guess."

"You *guess*?" She seemed very unsteady on her feet. Her voice sounded hysterical and mean. "It's going to rain! Have you ever fucked in the rain? Your teacher likes to fuck in the rain!"

"Jesus, Carol."

"He likes to fuck in the rain and he likes it on top of his desk and in cars and in other people's houses!"

By now people had accumulated, a circle of actors and actresses, a few passersby, no faculty or fellow academic deans, I hoped, everyone gathered to relish the spectacle of Carol crying, "I was going to have a baby! This man wouldn't let me have our baby!"

Billy, I noticed, wore a surprisingly composed (though somewhat glassed-over) expression, as if he were accustomed to violent exhibitionism in adults. He looked as though nothing could be more natural to him than a drunken woman's fury.

"I'm sorry, son," I said to the boy when Carol eventually ceased yelling. I had the uneasy feeling that I was in some way giving an expert rendering of Billy's real father, a man who must've been lacking—if our episode on the college lawn could be used as an indicator—backbone.

"It's cool," sighed Billy.

Then the rain came. The first drops were followed by wind and a great, rolling thunderclap. Tree branches swayed, and faeries scampered down from their platforms; then forked lightning struck nearby and the sky was instantly, ghostly white. Cast and crew began racing off in different directions. It was one of those thoroughly drenching gales that mark the beginning of summer—there was no point trying to stay dry. I reached out and took Carol by the arm, to comfort her and steady her. Rainwater soaked her hair and matted it in clumps. "Let's go indoors and get you wrapped in a warm towel," I shouted over the thunder; and she tugged her arm away and staggered to the edge of Puck's hole. She gave me one of her powerful, inimitable, disgusted looks, then leaned over, braced herself with her hands on her knees, and vomited into the pit. It happened quickly and was over before Billy or I could respond in a helpful way. A couple of heaves and Carol spat out the last. She looked terrible, like a witch in the Scottish play, I thought, or one of those modern descendants of crones on heaths, the living dead who climb from graves in horror movies. She was intensely drunk, of course. To Billy—she was looking mostly at the boy, though presumably Carol was thinking of me, or maybe neither Billy nor me—she said, "Look at you. You make me sick. You're like your father. He does whatever he wants with people. He's a shit. There's no love in this family."

Then she reeled away across the green. Billy and I watched Carol lurch around a corner and disappear behind Lunbeck Hall; then we turned, flustered and embarrassed, two men sharing a burden of humiliation, and walked together in the opposite direction. Rain was in our faces and our hands were buried in our pockets. Wind and water forced our eyes downward. Our shoes squished. Puddles were everywhere.

It was Billy who spoke first. "I doubt if I could run like that if I'd just barfed."

This comment made me like young Valentine immensely. I told him, "You should have played Puck."

This was said not so much to avoid the subject of Carol, her outburst and her vomiting, as to assuage feelings of guilt and shame by making an offering of some kind, however small and meaningless. Billy replied, in the right spirit, "Demetrius rocks."

"I'm glad you feel that way, Billy. Do you have any more of that good, strong dope?" I asked, dripping.

"No, sir. Not on me."

"That's too bad." For reasons I could not name, I went on: "When I was younger, I figured I'd grow up and get married and have children. But now years have gone by, and I'm not young."

"That's cool," said Billy. And he said, "Anyway, you shouldn't marry someone with a drinking problem."

"You're right about that."

"Mr. Barry?"

"Reg."

"Reg, do you think she knows about my father?"

"Knows what? She wasn't talking about your father. She thought I was your father, and you were our son that we never had, and you were growing up to be like me."

"That's crazy."

"Yes," I agreed. But it was true that I'd had the same notion as Carol. "See you tomorrow, Billy."

"Later, Reg."

Rehearsal, however, was not to be, not the next day, or the day after that, or the afternoon following. The storm worsened over the course of the first night, causing trees to fall on power lines, disabling phones and cutting off electricity to homes and college buildings. Classes were canceled. By morning of the second day, Tuesday, the thunder and lightning had stopped, though the sky remained gray, pouring heavy rain. The country around here is veined with creeks; these grew into deep, fast-moving rivers. The college, safe on high ground, operated minimally on generators. A party spirit prevailed. New couples would subsequently date their union to the week of the flash flood. The disaster occurred on Thursday, when natural dams in the nearby hills gave way, releasing torrents of water derived primarily from melted winter snow. The water crashed down into the valleys, washing away roads, trees, cars, and about twenty people. The National Guard and the International Red Cross landed helicopters on the Wm. T. Barry Gymnasium parking lot. Student volunteers collected cast-off clothing, canned food, blankets, etc. A short time later, it was learned that Harrison P. Mackay, a chemistry professor with forty years at the college, had been a flood casualty. The professor, not well known to me except as a red-faced personage wearing a bow tie, was found lodged in an embankment near the town of Chesterford. An emergency meeting of deans and the president convened; sadness was expressed and a few important memories were recalled. After the meeting, President Farnham took me aside and said, "Reginald, I want you to do that play if the weather clears. Right after our service for Harrison. We're all going to need cheering up."

It was in this way that we came to perform *A Midsummer Night's Dream* on a wet field before an audience of mourners wearing black.

"We're going to have a tough house," I said to my young company on the evening of the show.

Folding chairs were set up on the mushy ground. Organ music, a gloomy Episcopalian dirge, drifted in from the church at the college green's distant end. Harrison's memorial, under way. Skies remained partly cloudy, and a light breeze blew from the south. Together we stood, cast and crew, in a circle around Puck's hole. We weren't holding hands, though we should have been—there was a noticeable feeling, in the group, of apprehension, a communal dread and excitement only partly attributable to normal stage fright. The hole, in the wake of the week's rains, was a muddy pond. A duck, possibly blown far from home in the high winds a few days earlier, paddled on the surface. Fallen leaves looked like twisted miniature lily pads. These elements—water, duck, vegetation—combined to create a disturbingly powerful scene, a vastly reduced water vista that stood in relation to actual lakes as an artist's easel studies do to fully realized, complex paintings. It was, in other words, an excellent stage-set pond, not at all unlike a classical folly from an English garden, scaled down, deceptively simple, unreal enough to seem mysterious, primordial, sad.

The funeral music was not helping my mood. Jim Ferguson, our sexually aggressive Oberon and a zoology major, pointed out, "That's a female mallard. She's injured. Look at her—she's all crooked."

It was true. The duck listed in the water. Jim explained, "Ducks are vicious when they're hurt. They host human influenza and other dangerous viruses."

"Duck?" asked Martin Epps, waving his cane, straying precariously near the water's edge.

I told him, "Don't worry about the duck, okay?" To the cast in general, I said, "I'll need a couple of volunteers to lower Martin into the water when the time comes."

"Water?" said Martin, splashing with his cane, poking to find the hole's bottom.

The duck paddled weakly. All around me, kids in little groups stared down at it and smoked in that self-consciously erotic way—the dramatic puffs and the stagy, side-of-the-mouth exhalations blown upward into the air like steam escaping so many hot engines—that seems to be an advertisement for the carefree life. I couldn't take it. "Do you kids think you're going to live forever?" I shouted at these innocents. "Do you think life is some kind of *holiday*? You think that one day you'll stop being depressed! You won't *ever* stop being depressed! No matter how much *sex* you have!"

As if on cue, bells rang out from the chapel spire. Big wooden doors were flung open, and the first few mourners emerged from the church.

"Places!" cried Danielle.

Faeries tossed away cigarette butts and Royals crouched behind bushes while Mechanicals popped open their first-act beers. Billy Valentine passed Mary Victoria Frost an enormous joint. Martin Epps alone remained before his watery lair. "Billy, Mary, give me a hand with Martin," I said. "One, two, three." Up went the blind boy. He was light for a fat kid. He entered the water and said, "Ahhh."

"Stay put and don't piss off the duck," I directed him.

Billy and Mary and I crawled beneath the stage-left shrubs. Billy was about to stash the joint when I stopped him. "Hey, don't put that away. I need a hit." Fireflies blinked on, off, on. The audience settled into seats. Sounds of weeping rose from the house. I peeked up and could see, above me, faeries' legs dangling from platforms in trees, pair after pair of young legs.

"Good dope," I whispered to Billy.

Then Danielle gave the signal, and Greg Lippincott walked onstage and exclaimed, "Now, fair Hippolyta, our nuptial hour draws on apace; four happy days bring in another moon." Who can listen to that kind of stuff? A moment later came the cue for the young lovers to stumble out and stand before their elders. There was not much ground to stand on, only slippery grass beside the hole, where Martin was sunk in black water to his chin. The crooked duck regarded Martin with crazed eyes. "Full of vexation come I, with complaint against my child, my daughter Hermia," growled Egeus, as faculty, alumni, and a few undergraduates and parents wept tears for Harrison Mackay. Understandably, I felt the need to get a laugh. "The course of true love never did run smooth," I proclaimed morosely, and at that instant the duck began flapping its maimed wings, and Martin waved his cane wildly, and a gust of wind blew in like a sneeze from God, shaking the trees and blowing hats off heads in the audience. I looked for

Carol among the mourners. Where was she? Did she truly love me enough to have a child with me?

"It's going pretty well, don't you think?" I asked Billy when we came offstage at the middle of act one. We listened respectfully as Helena rattled off her famous speech about being sexually unattractive; and then Bottom and his men took over, rushing out and tackling one another and flubbing their lines—but it didn't matter what they did, because these characters are probably the most indestructible comic team in all of English literature, and, sure enough, when Bottom crunched Lion in the windpipe with his weight belt the audience let out its first decent belly laugh of the night. Billy and I hid behind the backstage trees and waited to run out, lie down to sleep on the cold ground, get drugged by Puck, wake up with our hard-ons, and begin chasing each other and/or Mary Victoria Frost and/or Sheila Tannenbaum through the haunted woods. Billy whispered, "Can I talk to you, Reg?"

"Call me Lysander during the show."

"I didn't want you to think, after the other day, you know, that I don't love my father."

He seemed maudlin, not at all like a happy comedian eager to chew the scenery. "I didn't think that. I'm sure you love your father very much," I assured him.

Saying this made me sad. Billy told me, "My father is not a bad man, no matter what people say."

Night was falling; the air had grown cold. Puck on his stomach crawled up the bank of his pond, then splashed back down into the water. Faeries on platforms jumped up and down noisily. Mary and Sheila, one tree over from me and Billy, adjusted costumes and each other's hair. Up Puck came again, covered in mud. His glasses had slipped from his head, and now his sightless eyes stared wildly; he could not have realized how afraid he looked. "I'll put a girdle. Round about. *Earth*—" he sputtered as, suddenly, the duck attacked. Martin howled and grasped at the mud and the grass, reaching for a handhold on dry land. It was too late. The duck blasted off the pond and came down hard in a spray of foam on Martin's pudgy, naked back. Webbed feet slapped the boy's white skin as the duck gave the coup de grâce with a thrust of her bill into Martin's neck.

"Thanks for talking, Lysander," Billy exclaimed. He bolted from behind our oak tree. Sheila Tannenbaum leaped out of hiding and ran after him. "I love thee not, therefore pursue me not," the boy yelled at the girl.

What is more exciting than kinetic, technical theater, the impeccable orchestrations of pratfall farce? I say this in consideration of the fact that audience members were leaving their seats and sneaking close, the better to gawk at Puck in his hole. As is always the case during productions of the Bard, a few carried paperback copies of the script. Sticklers. I watched them thumb pages back and forth, no doubt searching for references to a vengeful mallard. I have no objection to the public encroaching on the players—during Shakespeare's time, spectators sat on the stage and became, to a limited degree, implicated in the theater experience—but in this instance a participatory audience was a safety hazard. Billy, Mary, Sheila, and I had to dodge and weave throughout the better part of acts two and three. Darting barefoot and more or less naked around people wearing formal clothes had, as an activity, a distinctly anarchic, rebellious aspect—rebellious in the sense that it created, for me at least, the kind of sweaty excitement that comes with dangerous play. I felt free and young. I should say that I felt myself backsliding to a younger state of mind. It's hard to say what this feeling consisted in—panic and hope, disappointment, shame. I was wearing torn Barry Bears gym shorts and feeling like a teenager and running fast, and my feet sank into the earth, and mud splashed my legs. What is more awful and disorienting than adolescence? How had I become so lost and alone? What had persuaded me that I could play a young man's part? Was Billy pursuing me? Was I pursuing Billy? The bereaved came forward into the fray with heads bowed, and I stumbled through a puddle and narrowly missed crashing into President Farnham. "Reginald! This is criminal! Criminal!" the man shouted after me. Then: "Up and down, up and down, I will lead them up and down; I am fear'd in field and town: Goblin, lead them up and down," Martin Epps sang out magnificently, beautifully, before, at long last, he slid through ooze and disappeared, cane and all, beneath the water.

Bubbles, then silence.

Women and men wearing black lined the banks of the wine-black lake. They appeared, I thought, to be enjoying the show. It must be said that Shakespeare's genius lies partly in his plays' ready adaptability to the kinds of high-handed, decadent concepts guaranteed to astonish playgoers and offend the critics. Theater artistes often speak of their disregard for the audience, and it's a badge of integrity among some in this business to ignore the ostensible needs and desires of that inexpert class the ticket holders. But I think this is a rotten attitude. I'm in favor of putting on a show people will remember and talk about.

Who cared if it was too dark out to really see anything? Who noticed that Mary Victoria Frost was whacked on pot and dropping her best lines? What did it matter if Mustardseed and Moth had stripped off their G-strings in order to sixty-nine atop the tree-house stage set? Puck had sunk, and the important middle acts were nearing conclusion, and this meant it was time for me to cuddle on the grass with Sheila Tannenbaum.

There she was. She looked darling in her black-and-orange cheerleader's outfit and her mesh tights. She was my Helena, and she came toward me, smiling her awkward smile; and we settled on the wet ground and held each other in the night.

It was time for sleep. Sheila, the Lady Bears basketball star, snuggled warmly in my arms. She made a surprisingly good fit. She rested her head on my shoulder, and we kissed, lightly, and I looked up at trees and saw naked children.

How nice to lie on the grass. Other players, the demons and mere mortals, coupled nearby. It was a world of youthfulness and love. It was our summer at last. Faeries in the old oaks cradled Bottom and their mistress, and you could hear Sam English braying in ecstasy.

Beneath a tree, sprawled face down on the ground, lay Mary Victoria Frost, my poor Hermia. She looked so pale, so stuporous.

There would be plenty of time, later in act four or five or whatever act this was, to wake up, dump Helena, and marry, for a fitting consummation, the right girl.

It was the deep of night, late even for the fireflies. A few appeared here and there. Soon they would be gone. In the meantime, the Lord of Athens lit a cigarette and waited in the wings.

POND, WITH MUD

The yellow bird made from cloth and / vines sits better in the / window than / the red truck I built last / year of / bottles," Patrick Rouse wrote, in the fifteenth volume of what he liked to refer to as his life's work—in reality, a journal crammed with passages written in a metaphorized terminology that Patrick had borrowed, or so he told himself, from the Imagist poets, and which he used to describe his emotions and whatever objects aroused his emotions. The "yellow bird," for instance, referred to a lingerie bikini set featuring yellow lace woven in a tropical-jungle motif, which he had purchased a few days earlier for his fiancée, Caroline, who, at that moment, was standing in the living room modeling it for Patrick and—though the boy could hardly appreciate the significance of his mother's erotic poses in bare feet before the hearth . . . or *could* he?—for her son, the "three-eyed rabbit." That being, of course, more of Patrick's code, or poetry, in this case describing Gregory, Caroline's five-year-old from her marriage to Roger, an unemployed chamber musician.

"You like it?" Caroline asked Patrick.

He did. He did like it! He said, "That's a good color for you."

Caroline turned and peered over her shoulder, as if into a

mirror hung on the wall. There was no mirror. She drank from her wine, and said, "It *is* a good color, isn't it? I wouldn't have picked it, because it's bright. But you spotted it! You had the wisdom to see it." She took another sip.

"Not wisdom," Patrick said, as he wrote, in scratchy blue letters on a blank page in the book open on his lap, "Fat airplanes spot cloudless skies / their propellers / soft fans humming / leaking," which was effectively a reminder to himself that soon he would be taking off his clothes, getting into bed, pushing aside the blue coverlet, climbing atop Caroline, and fucking.

"You always know what colors I can wear."

"All I need to figure that out is a peek in the closet."

At that point Gregory, who was sitting in the enormous Mission-style chair beneath the framed photograph of Caroline on vacation, waving from the bow of the USS *Wisconsin*— Gregory made one of his demands.

"Other! Chair!"

"Do you want to get him?" Patrick said.

"You get him. I've got these new things on."

What was difficult was not moving the boy from one chair to another, exactly; the problem consisted in the likelihood that, once moved, Gregory might become sad. It was grotesque, Patrick thought, always to be hoisting this growing boy, who could, after all, walk. Why did they do it, he and Caroline? Why did they take orders from Gregory? There was nothing wrong with him—at least, nothing Dr. Percy could ever find.

"Here I come, my young boy who is not my own," Patrick said. It was one of his jokes. He closed the volume on his lap and capped his pen, an ostentatious black-and-red lacquered fountain pen that he had bought for himself as a gift, and which leaked while he wrote. As always, he checked his hands, his shirt, and the front of his pants around the zipper. He found no ink smears. It had been a good writing day.

It frequently happened, when Patrick stopped purposefully making notes in "Pond, with Mud" (his secret name for his encrypted journal), that he began to feel as if he might be on the verge of formulating a concrete idea about the nature of existence, and about his place in the scheme of things. It was a feeling that came, as he thought of it, from deep in his heart. But each time he got this feeling it almost instantly went away. Would he never know what it was that he was trying to think about himself?

He forced himself to concentrate on Gregory. The boy was spread, neither sitting nor lying—Gregory was doing a perverse version of both at once—across the leather seat cushion of the big Stickley that Patrick had carted with him everywhere he'd lived since college. The chair was coming apart in places. Something structural somewhere had broken, and one leg had a tendency to work its way gradually loose from the frame. Every now and then, the leg had to be slapped back into position. Patrick had seduced Amy in this chair. Then Vanessa. Then Caroline.

He said to the sprawling boy, "Funny Bunny, I'm going to do something for you that you are going to like."

"Don't get him excited," Caroline said. She placed her wineglass on the mantel. She did a slow, balletic turn, showing Patrick her body. And Patrick knew—her voice had that angry sound—that the wine had begun to take hold.

He approached the boy. He leaned over and placed his hands under Gregory's arms. He began to lift. He said, "Do you love it when I hold you in the air? Are you *my* Bunny?"

In fact, the approval Patrick cared for was Caroline's. Patrick craved recognition from her, in order to view himself favorably as a man who could function as a father. This had become especially meaningful to him after what had happened a few days before.

He had taken the afternoon off from his job at the printing press and gone with the boy in tow to catch the two o'clock train to the zoo that had recently opened on the outskirts of town, on marshlands that had been home to a chemical-solvent extraction plant that had burned to the ground. Immediately following the zoo's inaugural ribbon-cutting ceremony—or relatively soon after, to be more precise—strange things had begun to happen to the more esoteric wild animals. Why was it that the rare and endangered species, the ones you'd never heard of, all seemed to have compromised immune systems? At any rate, it had been reported in the papers that the board of governors and the director of the zoo were soon to come under indictment for cruelty to animals and for various mis-appropriations of municipal funds. The zoo's future was in question. The time for a visit was now.

"Here we go!" Patrick had exclaimed to Gregory as, with the boy's damp hand grasped in his fist, the two of them made their way awkwardly through one of the angling, cavernous passageways leading from the street to the elevated central lobby of the city's restored art deco train terminal. Patrick was in the habit of carrying along, wherever he went, the current volume of "Pond, with Mud." Here, with a view ahead toward the train station's towering and heavily leaded windows, win-dows that allowed ray after ray of sunlight to spill into the station's airy middle spaces, illuminating floating dust and giv-ing the whole marble place the steamy, mystical aura of a site associated with feelings and moods that were, for want of a better word, spiritual (the spirit of progress? This, to Patrick, had the feel of a *theme*), even otherworldly—here in the train station, Patrick felt inspired to say to the boy, whose hand he now shook loose, "Hang on a minute, Bunny."

He took his pen from the inside pocket of his coat. He

unscrewed the brass-and-lacquer cap. What he loved most about untwisting the cap was the care required to keep the ink from running. Rituals were important. For instance, Patrick always carried the journal tucked at a certain angle beneath his left arm, pressed close to his heart, in the manner, he fantasized, of some boyish scholar traipsing with a rare edition of Donne through an English library hung with tapestries. Now he opened the volume and found a clean page. He gazed up at the tile mosaics of women's faces adorning the lintels above the station windows. As he wrote, Patrick whispered to himself, in cadence with the travelers' footsteps echoing along the entryway to the great hall, "Beasts or angels / arcing / entwined."

"We! Go!" Gregory shouted, badly interrupting Patrick, who looked rapidly left to right, and up and down, saying, "What? What? Of course, Gregory. We're going to the zoo to see the deformed animals."

Patrick had one of his upsetting everyday thoughts: Christ, I'm not much of a poet, am I? He pushed this question out of his mind.

In a soft voice, and in tones meant to be conciliatory, he said to Gregory, "Hey, little man, you don't have to scream."

It was too late. The boy was crying. Patrick shut the book. He had forgotten to blow the ink dry, and the page would smudge. It would be a bad writing day.

"Shit," he said to Caroline's son, bawling in the middle of the crowded station concourse. Carefully Patrick capped and returned the pen to the interior pocket of his jacket. He produced a wad of the loose tissues he always carried in his coat pockets for these routine weeping sessions. He knelt and pushed the soft white paper toward the boy's face. What had made him think that he could ever deal with a kid?

In fact, he *was* dealing with a kid, and not doing nearly as bad a job as he worried others might suppose, were any of those people rushing by—on their way to trains or jobs—to stop and watch as he wiped the tears and the snot from Gregory's cheeks and the rashy area around his mouth.

"There, it's all right. Come on. Don't you want to see the goiters on the chimpanzees?"

"The! What?"

"Where in the world did you learn to talk, anyway?" Patrick asked. This question came out sweetly. He said, "We're a pair, aren't we?" and finished wiping the boy's face. Gregory had such clear eyes. They were not at all bloodshot, even after sobbing.

Patrick put the wet tissues back in a coat pocket to dry for the next squall. From another pocket he fished a child-size bottle of juice and a miniature straw. He shook the bottle, opened it, planted the straw in the juice, and held bottle and straw for Gregory to drink. The bottle was quite small; Patrick's hand closed around it. Were you to have seen the two of them, the man kneeling before the boy, the boy sucking on the almost invisible plastic straw, you might have imagined that the boy was drinking from the man's hand.

"Ready?" Patrick asked.

"Juice!" Gregory exclaimed, and, just like that, he was done drinking, and everything returned to normal.

Patrick removed the wet straw from the juice. He capped the bottle and put it back in his pocket for later. No trash can was in sight, so he replaced the straw in the jacket pocket already stuffed with the bottle and the used tissues. Looking over the top of Gregory's head, he saw, across the terminal crowded with people indistinctly coming and going, a young man and woman holding hands and running, though not in the manner of people hurrying to board a train. The girl seemed to be skipping, or dancing. Her skirt flew up around her legs. Was there music playing in her head? Was she maybe wearing headphones?

Patrick took Gregory's hand in his. He said, with equal measures of sarcasm and earnestness, "Shall we dance?"

It was at this moment that a musician who had set up near the door to the street—the door through which Patrick and Gregory had entered the station—began playing a violin. The musician was situated directly behind Patrick, who, for one narcissistic moment, believed that the music in the tunnel was a reverberant production of his own imagination. Then, peering down at Gregory, he saw that Gregory was peeking around his, Patrick's, legs. Gregory was *seeing* the man playing the violin. Patrick turned and saw that the violinist was Roger, Gregory's father, the man Caroline had been married to when Patrick had come on the scene.

"Roger! Hey, Roger!" Patrick called down the corridor. It was an act of impulsiveness and guilt. Patrick heard his own voice echoing, decaying, and dying against the richer, seductive sounds of the music. The musician—yes, it was Caroline's former husband—was wearing a green coat that looked frayed and unclean. God only knew what he might have been carrying in the pockets of that coat. It appeared that Roger had continued to be what he had been in the old days: a poor, alcoholic artist.

"Look, Bunny," Patrick said to the top of Gregory's head. "Do you know who that man is?"

"Daddy."

"Right you are. Daddy. The pea-green boat with torn sails. Someone should haul her out to sea."

What was he saying? What was he *doing*? Why had he called out? Had the violinist heard? Had Roger seen Gregory spying from behind Patrick's legs? Patrick flipped open "Pond, with Mud," got out his pen, went through the ritual of delicately removing the cap, and scribbled (after searching for an unsmudged page) a few lighthearted, comical-nautical associations. "Pea-green / boat / towed / in shreds / out." This time he remembered to blow on the ink.

And it was still possible, he thought, that Roger had neither seen nor heard them, that he and the boy might slip away and take refuge on a train-platform bench, before setting out on their journey to the contaminated zoo. He had taken the afternoon off for this. They really ought to make it to the zoo.

He watched the violinist, who was swaying above the hips in that enchantedly theatrical fashion in which string players expectably do—as if blowing in the intermittent wind on which all music travels. And travelers, actual ones, entering and departing through the colossal wooden doors onto the street, altered their courses, automatically tacking around Roger and his empty music case left open on the ground for small bills and change. Patrick watched the bow rising and falling, pulled by the violinist's hand across the instrument's strings. He had the impression that the musician was rocking himself to sleep. The music rolled up the tunnel. Because the corridor walls and the ceiling were tiled, the notes came on amplified, and certain passages sounded both muddled and complexly dynamic, orchestral.

It was Brahms. No, it wasn't. It was Sibelius. No, it was Robert Schumann. It was not Mendelssohn—that much was evident, even to Patrick. And it was not, on second thought, Schumann. It was Brahms. Roger had had a thing for Brahms.

Roger was looking toward them now, peering up the hundred feet of windowless tunnel that separated him from Patrick and Gregory. Even at this distance, Patrick, gazing back down the dirty white corridor, could see where Gregory had come by his big damp eyes.

Patrick and the three-eyed rabbit stood watching Roger watch them. Now and then, people wearing backpacks or maneuvering wheeled suitcases came between them. The oncoming people pressed down on Patrick and the boy, and

Gregory wrapped his arms around Patrick's leg. What was interesting about this moment was the way in which Roger's playing produced an occasion for what felt to Patrick like a bond between the men—it was music for male affinity, for courtship, for sharing—and, furthermore, between the men and the boy. Would Roger understand this? Gregory's real parents, that early afternoon before the trip to visit the dying animals, were not Roger and Caroline, or even Patrick and Caroline, but Patrick and Roger.

"I guess we ought to say hello," Patrick said to Gregory. "Come on, Bunny, let go of my leg."

"Can't!"

"Yes, you can. Knock it off." He had to reach down and pull the boy off him. He anticipated tears, but in fact he was the one who felt like crying. This feeling came on suddenly. He said, "I'm going to pick you up. You'll be safe and happy in the air! Are you ready to be happy?"

"Up!"

"Good boy. Let's say hi to your daddy, and after that we'll ride out to the zoo and see something tragic."

Was he crazy? They'd never make their train this way. He knelt before the boy. Patrick held the journal in one hand. Now he reached behind Gregory, pressing the journal between his arm and Gregory's back. His other hand went beneath Gregory's arm. He got a grip on Gregory. He stood and brought the boy close to him, squeezing him with "Pond, with Mud." He would have preferred to avoid carrying Gregory. Once up, the kid would be unwilling to go down. And lately he'd got heavy.

If only Caroline had been with them. On the other hand, though, maybe not. In truth, it occurred to him, he didn't want Caroline there at all.

"Wait a minute, hold on, wait a minute," he said to the Funny Bunny. There was something Patrick had to get down in the work-in-progress, before he forgot. It was about Caroline. He pictured her dressed for the office, with her scarf knotted over the buttoned top button of her starched white shirt, noosing her neck. Why had Patrick never before considered that knotted scarf in relation to the death of love? The scarf produced such obvious imagery. Obvious? Not *too* obvious.

What to do? How to get words down on paper? If he lowered the Bunny to the ground, there could be a tantrum and the day would be ruined. On the other hand, were he to try to open the book and take out the pen—well, forget it, it was out of the question. Could he persuade Gregory to climb up and ride on his shoulders, and in this way free his hands? But he wouldn't have free hands, would he? He'd be holding Gregory's knees, restraining Gregory from kicking him in the chest with the heels of his little rubber sneakers.

He carried Gregory down the tiled hall, against the rush of people entering from the street. He felt afraid. Why, all of a sudden, was he so full of fear? He knew the answer. It was simple. He wasn't making his art. No, that wasn't the complete answer. The complete answer was that he was not an artist. He was a person who let language dissolve into nothingness. Did that qualify as an insight?

Walking along the train-station tunnel, the boy cradled in his arms, he felt as if he were pushing through music—as if the music from the violin had become resistant, like a substance.

"Hello!" Patrick said too loudly to the violinist. "Brahms!" he exclaimed. Why was he talking like the boy? What an idiot he was. He'd become submissive. The only way he could make things worse would be to pull dollar bills from his pocket and toss them into the violin case.

With one arm, he held Gregory. He dug deeply into his pants pocket. Money and old tissues were wadded in a ball in Patrick's pocket. He brought out a handful. There was no way

for him to count the money. He held it up before his eyes.
Twenties and fives.

"Gregory and I were on our way to the zoo! I took the
day off. We thought we could maybe see a few wild animals
before they have to quarantine them. That's a joke. I guess it's
not funny." And he said, "Right, Gregory? The zoo! Gregory,
say hello to your father." And with that he let a few bills flutter
from his hand to the case on the ground. It was probably thirty
or forty dollars.

Could anything have been meaner? Could he have been
more cruel? Here was a demonstration of the power of a weak
man over a weaker man. And there was more to come, when
he shoved the money and the tissues back into his pocket and
said, "Can I buy you a drink?" Patrick understood that he was
not so much abusing the other man as punishing himself; they
would drink together, the two men, and Patrick would buy,
and he would get drunk enough to give himself credit for being
a generous person. Later in the day, Roger might get up his
nerve and punch him; but if he did he might injure his hand
and be unable to play the violin for a while, and Patrick would
be obliged to help him with a loan. There was no end to it.

"Drink?" the violinist said. Immediately he stopped playing and knelt to stow away his violin. He took care securing
it in the case, but was speedy nonetheless. He needs a drink,
Patrick thought. Patrick felt misgivings as he watched the
violin-case lid come down over money that had recently been
his. Roger snapped the case shut and stood up, and, a moment
later, Gregory and his two fathers set out to waste the day sitting on stools in a dark train-station bar, a place off to the
side, away from the sunlight, and populated with men who
leaned down hard and unspeaking over their glasses.

There was no music in the bar. The place looked to Patrick
as if it had been neglected by the architects who had recently completed the renovation of the train station. Had

they forgotten about it? It had a linoleum floor and, in keeping with the historical standards for furnishings in these sorts of haunts, red vinyl booths, and walls painted a dark shade down low, toward the floor, and a lighter color up above. The ceiling was yellowing; certainly in another age, the seventies most likely, it had been white. All those burning cigarettes. All those people coughing themselves to death. Patrick imagined the dark bar full of coughers. There was something about the smell in the place, too. It smelled to Patrick like a hospital, or, faintly, like Roger, except saltier. This bar off to the side of the concourse was all that was left of the old train station; it reminded Patrick of the periods in modern literature when a decline in civilization is evident in the works of the poets. But when he thought about this he could not dream up any original lines that did not refer to cigarettes, or to the fact that lit cigarettes held in the air by drunks in dark rooms become little galaxies, spiraling.

Roger threw his violin case on the bar. This was a powerful move on his part. It showed that he had confidence in what he trusted (the hard case) to protect what he needed (the fragile violin) in order to maintain for himself some small place in which he could be a—what? A man in the world.

Patrick settled Gregory on a stool. Then, in an imitation of Roger's confidence, he threw "Pond, with Mud" on the bar. This was a cavalier and companionable gesture. There would be time later to compose formal impressions regarding the experience of chucking his literary work around. In the meantime, he felt in his coat pocket for the fountain pen. There it was, clipped to the pocket's lining.

The bartender came over. Roger asked for a beer.

"Sure thing, Roger," the bartender said to him. "How's it going today?"

"Money!"

"Good for you."

This short conversation emboldened Patrick to order a drink suitable for the occasion. What *was* the occasion? And never mind that Scotch had been his father's drink. In memory, Patrick could see the old man with a drink in his hand, inhaling from his cigarette in the night. Frankly, there came a point in each and every day when Patrick saw this image of his father.

"May I have a Scotch and soda?"

"Anything for the little guy?" the bartender asked, and, for a moment, Patrick was not sure what the man was talking about. He thought the bartender was referring to him—to Patrick. Little guy? Patrick caught on and said, "I'm carrying juice."

He hauled the juice out of his coat pocket. He shook the bottle. He reached back into his pocket, got the miniature straw, and wiped it with a bar napkin. While wiping, he said, "Roger, I like your playing." Where were those drinks? Patrick looked at Gregory and said, "How are you doing on that stool, Bunny? Comfortable? We can move over to a booth as soon as one opens up. Please don't cry."

"Bunny?" This from Roger.

"We call him that. Actually, we don't call him that. I call him that. Right, Bunny? Are you my Funny Bunny?" Patrick had the juice ready. He held the bottle for Gregory to drink. Gregory, somehow managing to keep his balance on the elevated barstool, leaned over between the two men, took the straw expertly in his mouth, and, with his hair falling forward over his ears, hiding his face, began to suck.

Patrick said, "Yeah, good boy."

"Yeah! Boy," Roger exclaimed. Who was submissive now?

The drinks came, and Patrick put his money on the bar. Roger got his beer, and Patrick his Scotch; Gregory worked on his miniature juice; the three of them drank together. It

was a moment of harmony produced—in that cosmic dark-
ness that made the forlorn station bar a place apart from
the world—by alcohol, the absence of women, and, Patrick
thought, love.

"Shall we have another?" he asked.

"Another," Roger answered.

"Here's to being here," Patrick said, hoisting his glass; and
he had the feeling, as he made this toast, that there were all
manner of things he wanted to say (and had for some time
needed to say, now that he thought about it) to Roger. For instance, Patrick suddenly couldn't wait to assure Roger that he
and Caroline had been very upset when they'd discovered that
he had lost his job teaching at the conservatory. But how to say
this in words that would not be hurtful to the man's pride?
Also, was it a good idea for Patrick to let the deposed husband
know that Caroline still cared for him? Was it wise for Patrick
to mention Caroline at all? He felt himself on the verge of telling Roger that he was sure that he, Patrick, might be able to
persuade Caroline to overlook a few of those child-custody
legalities. Bury the ax. No one ever need raise his arm and strike
anyone in anger again. Roger could drop by Patrick and Caroline's apartment, have a beer or a glass of wine, play a lullaby on
his fiddle, and hold his son for a few minutes. Roger didn't
look like a person who wanted to hurt a little boy. Did he?

It wasn't Patrick's place to make promises to Roger. It wasn't
his place to say anything to Roger.

Nonetheless he said, "Do you want to hold him?"

Patrick drank from his drink. In that instant, he felt at
peace with himself—he could understand drinking. Caroline
did not like Patrick to drink. Correction: Caroline didn't like
him to drink *too much*. It occurred to him then that the an-
niversary of their engagement was coming up in three days.
Jesus! He had to think about a present.

The train-station bar was emptying. Patrick supposed that

the men in the bar were leaving to catch trains to the suburbs. Either that or heading back to their jobs. Every now and then, the door to the bar would open, and light would flood in, briefly. The person leaving might stand silhouetted in this bright light, waving a hand at the drinkers left behind.

"So long. See you tomorrow," the bartender called toward the door as it closed. The light disappeared, and the bartender brought Patrick and Roger one beer and one Scotch. He counted out money from the pile in front of Patrick. The money was wet, and there was tissue paper mixed with it.

"Do you want to hold him?" Patrick asked Roger again. "It's all right if you don't feel like it."

"No," Roger said to him.

"No? You don't? Or you do? Want to hold the Bunny?"

The bartender came back carrying change. He put the change on the bar. "Will you be wanting anything for your little boy? Will you be wanting a glass of milk?"

Was the bartender addressing Patrick? Or Roger? Gregory had stopped drinking from the juice bottle and was leaning over against the rounded edge of the bar, his head pillowed on arms crossed beneath him, in the manner, and with the posture, of a child slumbering at a school desk. His eyes were closed. The juice was empty.

"He's doing fine, we're all fine, we're great, thank you," Patrick said. Patrick was drunk. Being drunk, he wondered why he was not more often drunk. Was that right? Grammatically speaking? Not more often drunk?

"You let me know," the bartender said.

To Roger, Patrick said, "Gregory is tired. We should let him rest a minute. You can hold him later."

Gregory's real father had already finished his beer, Patrick noticed. How many did that make? In all? As for Patrick, he was not, when he spoke, slurring his words, though he feared he might slur his words were he not careful not to. Something like that. Between the two men, the boy slept. These two grown men gazed at each other through the dark, across the boy; and Patrick found himself wondering how old Roger was. Caroline had told him, but he couldn't remember. In Roger's eyes, Patrick saw the boy's eyes. Roger's face might or might not have been a predictor of the face Gregory would one day show to the world. Roger was unshaven, with hair growing down his neck, past the top of his shirt collar, which was unbuttoned to the third button, and lay open beneath the pea-green coat that needed cleaning, and which was either too large or too small for Roger—it was hard for Patrick to say which. The effect was tacky. No, "tacky" wasn't the right word. Roger's chest was white and skinny, the chest of a man who'd begun drinking before he was a man. And the tip of his nose was red—a red nose! Like Gregory, Roger had a rashy mouth. Whiskers went this way and that. His hair looked lifeless.

He could play the violin, though. Boy, could he! That was a hell of a lot more than Patrick could do!

Was it time yet to relocate from the bar to a booth? The barstools weren't the most comfortable things.

"Bartender!" Patrick called. "Hit us!" And to Roger he said, "This is going to have to be it. I'm about out of cash."

The men looked sadly at the money. It was true, there wasn't much left. Would Roger offer to spend the money that Patrick had dropped in his case? It was not likely.

And, hey, where was "Pond, with Mud"? Had the bartender taken it and stashed it behind the bar? Had one of the miserable drunks walked off with it? No, there it was, next to the violin. It was safe.

To Roger, Patrick said, "You've hardly said a word all night. All day. My friend. Tell me something. I've told you things. I've told you that Bunny and I are on our way to the zoo. I've told you we were going to look at all the crazy animals. I've told you that you can hold your son. I want you to tell me something I can write down. Tell *me* something, fucker," he said to Roger, and immediately regretted this. "I'm sorry. I am sorry."

"Don't," the other man said.

Don't? Don't what? Don't be sorry? Don't say these things? Don't apologize? Don't ask Roger to apologize?

Roger placed his hand on Gregory's back. He moved his hand gently, stroking the boy. As Patrick watched this, it came into his mind to say, "Don't wake him." Another "don't." Was that what Roger had meant? Don't ask me not to touch my son?

"Gregory." Roger said his son's name. "Gregory."

The boy's face was wrinkled from lying against his arms and the edge of the bar. He was coming awake. How long had he been sleeping? What was the time? How could there be a bar without a clock?

Patrick removed his malfunctioning pen from his pocket. But by the time he'd got the pen out he'd forgotten his subject. His subject had been? What were his subjects? Patrick's subjects were the usual subjects. There was another of his unfunny jokes. Patrick's subject had been time. But he'd forgotten time. Why was he holding his pen? He put it away. Was it leaking? No, that wetness Patrick felt was water dripping on him from the bottom of his glass. How much had he drunk? Or maybe the wetness was a spot of ink soaking through the lining of his coat, staining his shirt above his heart.

And Patrick, unwilling or unable to allow himself to be vanquished by Roger, said, sharply, "Hey, everybody, I'm bleeding to death!"

That did it. That brought on the tempest. Could anything have hurt Patrick more than to hear the boy cry out at the sound of his, Patrick's, voice?

"No crying, Bunny. Okay, no crying? No need to cry. I'm

going to pick you up! You'll be happy in the air! Are you ready to be happy?"

He looked across at Gregory's father. One last look before leaving. He believed he knew in that instant what he saw in Roger's eyes.

And with that he leaned close to Gregory, picked up the Scotch and soda from the bar, raised the glass to the boy's lips, and said, "Here. Don't cry."

SOLACE

They were children of parents who'd acted grotesquely, some might say violently, toward them, even when they were fairly little, and when, in their early thirties, they met and began sharing confidences, their discovery of this common ground—for that was how she thought of it—seemed to her a great, welcome solace. At last! she thought more than once during the weeks and months after they'd started going to bed together—always at friends' places, because they were both in transitional periods and didn't have anywhere comfortably private; she was saving money by sleeping on a foldout sofa in the living room of a one-bedroom apartment in the East Twenties that she shared with her friend Susan, while he, also recently forced to cut expenses, was installed uptown in a rented room in the apartment of an older, intimidating former co-worker, also named Susan. At *last!* Jennifer said to herself many times before falling asleep after sex in some friend's or friend of a friend's freshly changed bed. Then she would squeeze his hand.

One morning after this way of life had been going on for a while—it was the day after the summer solstice, and they were occupying their sixth or seventh borrowed apartment, getting away from their Susans for the weekend—Christopher woke early. He pushed back the sheet and the thin bedspread, rolled off the strange mattress, and, leaving her sleeping, went searching for coffee in Bert and Lucie's kitchen. He moved down the line of melamine cabinets, opening and shutting the white doors. The open, uncurtained kitchen window gave him a view of a treeless back courtyard and neighbors' windows directly opposite. There was no breeze. Living without air-conditioning or blinds was, Christopher thought, exactly the kind of thing his friends Bert and Lucie would do; it was a statement about iconoclasm or freedom or hedonism, and there was more evidence of it, the ambiguous statement, everywhere in the apartment—in the preponderance of tacky objects from the sixties and seventies, in the bright upholstery colors on the couch and podlike chairs, in the large fish tank inhabited by a piranha.

Christopher put water on the stove and turned on the burner. There, on the counter beside the refrigerator, was the gin bottle. But where was the coffee? He was naked.

They'd met at the end of the previous winter, at a dinner party thrown by a movie producer for whom Christopher had once done some legal work. The producer's husband had been seated directly across the table from Christopher, and on the husband's right was Jennifer. Shortly after the halibut came out, Christopher remembered, this man had dropped his napkin on the floor beside her chair, then boldly leaned into her space to reach for it. As he reached down, his forehead bumped the side of her left breast. And that wasn't all. Coming up after grabbing the napkin, the husband, in a show of spatial awareness or perhaps a feigned considerateness, moved backward to avoid a second contact. Instead of sitting straight in his seat, however, he paused, his body bent awkwardly over, his face close to the breast, which he gazed at, it seemed to Christopher, with intensity. In a mock-formal voice, addressing the breast, the husband growled, "Pardon," then sat upright and laughed, forcing Jennifer to grimace out at the table as she shared the joke. But what was the joke?

"You're Charlie Harrison's friend!" she shouted at Christopher before coffee was served, before they pushed back their chairs and wandered off to find privacy—the sloppiness of the people around them making it possible for them to seek refuge with each other—in a bedroom.

"Charlie," he said, and finished chewing. Then he thought: Christ, why bring that up?

Down the table, a man who'd drunk too much knocked his glass across a plate, and there was a commotion.

"You've got to speak up!" she called over the noise. "I can't hear a word you're saying!"

"How do you know Charlie?" he asked loudly, and she yelled back, "I wouldn't say I *know* him!"

"I don't, either! I mean, I don't *not* know him! I *know* him"—gathering steam—"but, well, not *well*, anymore. I *knew* him!" What was he doing? Why was he blurting?

"I understand! I understand completely!" she shouted at him. "Here's to old acquaintances!" She leaned over her plate, raised her glass in her hand, and, in a softer voice, told him, "My name's Jennifer."

Was she making a toast? He had nothing in his glass but water. It occurred to him that she'd maybe had a bad experience with his ex-friend, that she and Charlie had possibly slept together. He tilted himself forward to meet her halfway. A candle burned between them, and he moved it aside. Her eyes were brown and somewhat cloudy; he made a point of looking into them when he said, "It's bad luck to toast with water."

"We don't want bad luck."

So he picked up a wineglass from among the scattered dishes, one that had been filled but seemed not to belong to anyone, and raised it to his mouth and took a quick fake

drink, even that a violation of the major rule he lived by, the
rule he tried not to violate too often or—since most nights he
was, after all, likely to break down—too early in the evening.
But it wasn't early in the evening, was it?

"For luck," he said.

Later, sitting next to him on a bed, atop partygoers' mixed-
up coats, scarves, and hats, she told him that she'd worked in
the film business for six years but hadn't felt at home, that
she'd wanted all along to paint. Her mother painted but had
never made a career of it, though who knew what might have
happened were it not for her mother's drinking and drugging.
Those were Jennifer's words: drinking and drugging. She
told him she felt sure that as a very young girl she'd probably
been happy, but because of things that had happened when
she was a bit older in her childhood, things that had influenced
every aspect of her existence—did he follow her meaning?—
those sweeter memories, whatever they might have been, were
no longer playing. Her current project was self-acceptance,
not an uncommon goal, she said, among the sorts of people
she mainly hung out with, people who'd moved to the city
from distant places because, as she put it, "they had no homes
in their home towns."

That last line sounded like something she'd said before,
on more than one occasion. Nonetheless, her words were a
mini-revelation to him. She'd expressed a condition that he'd
known in life yet had been unable to articulate until it was
figured forth concretely by her, in speech that sounded canned.
"I'm enjoying myself," he told her, and she said, "I'm having
a nice time, too. I'm glad I came tonight," and went on to tell
him how much her painting meant to her—so much that it
frightened her sometimes—even though she was only a be-
ginner. She was interested in realism, she said. This was one
area in which she differed from her mother, who, she confided
to Christopher in a low whisper, was an abstract expressionist;

and—she was getting excited again—the fact of her mother's frustrated ambition obviously had everything to do with the anxieties that she, Jennifer, felt whenever she picked up a paintbrush. Breathlessly, she told him, "I need to make painting mine."

"How about you?" she asked.

"Me?"

"Yes." Flirting. "You."

"I'm not an artist."

He paused. She waited. Finally he said, "I used to scribble a few lines in college. Poetry. Does that count?"

"Count? What do you mean, count?" She laughed, and he said, "Oh, I just, I guess, I don't know," and then, against his will, he was laughing with her, because what else could he do? He gazed at the side of her face, wondering, absurdly, whether he would like what he saw—what he would see—as the years rolled by and she and he got older. Her nose, it seemed to him, was on the small side in relation to her wide mouth. Makeup did not completely conceal a slight dryness to her skin, and her hair, pulled tightly back, gave her forehead a stretched appearance—would she look less startled without the ponytail? And yet she was attractive in a prim, smart way that he found sexy. And who was he to find fault, he with his thin upper lip and jutting ears?

After they'd stayed a while longer in their hosts' bedroom, she exclaimed, "I have to go now!" and leaped up and tugged her coat and scarf from the loose pile—he was forced to scramble when other guests' clothes began shifting beneath him. Would he walk her out? In fact, would he mind saying goodbye to the others for her? Yes, he assured her, he'd be happy to. Where were her gloves, though? she wanted to know. "Did you check in your coat? Are the gloves in a pocket? Are there pockets in the lining? Could the gloves be in the lining?" he asked. But they weren't there. Nor were they under

the bed. "They'll turn up," she announced as she marched
out of the bedroom. They sneaked past the clamorous guests
in the dining room. "Sh-h-h," he whispered in her ear, and
she giggled. He could smell her hair, a sweet smell of—what?
At the front door, they did not kiss.

This abruptness of hers during the moments leading to
leave-taking (was it that parting produced anxiety, or that her
mounting claustrophobia required a quick getaway?) was, as
Christopher would witness again and again, part of a style
characterized by a variety of impatient behaviors—dramatically
rolling her eyes, for instance, whenever it seemed to her that
he was being pathetic. They would be a wry couple. But a
little sarcasm, even in fun—and the evening had turned out
to be fun—a little sarcasm went a long way for Christopher,
who, when they next met, at a Village café appropriate for a
casual non-date (though it was, in fact, a big date for Christopher, in that it was his turn to risk a few remarks about his
own origins), told her, "Everybody laughed at me."

A week had passed since the dinner party.

"Everybody? Who's everybody?" She crossed her arms. She
was taking his measure. She wore a pink woolen scarf wrapped
loosely about her shoulders, in the style of young Parisian
women. At the rear of the café, a mother and her two small
children were making a racket. Christopher spoke up. "My
family. My family laughed at me," and immediately she broke
in, "I understand what you mean. Everybody who matters,"
and he replied, "Yeah, right?" before continuing, in tones
that she would learn to recognize as harbingers of a mild
paranoia, "For example, let's say I had something serious on
my mind, something to say at the dinner table. I'm trying to
think of an example. I can't think of one. It doesn't matter. I
could have been talking about anything. They'd burst out
laughing! It got so that I was afraid to speak! If I tried telling
a joke or a funny story—and I didn't often try that—they'd sit

in their chairs and chew their food. But I could read the obituaries, well, maybe not the obituaries, and my father and mother
and sisters would laugh!"

This made her laugh—*he'd* made her laugh. She could
just see the awful scene around the family table. Christopher
peeking over the top of the obituary page. She hoped her
laughter would be taken conspiratorially, as evidence of
her recognition of his mistreatment. And his shame.

At the back of the café, the mother struggled with her
children. Crying had begun. Jennifer turned to look. When
she finally turned back to Christopher, he said, "You see?
You laughed. It's so exasperating."

That was when she rolled her eyes. Was she playing with
him? He gazed down at his spoon and knife, at his empty cup
set crookedly on its saucer, at the miniature milk pitcher and
the sugar bowl. What was the use in telling her how bleak he
felt when people found him funny? What if he were to reach
across the table and touch her face? Right now. Would she
understand, through his touch, that making people laugh felt
to him like being hit? What made people want to hit him in
this way?

He said, "It's not your fault."

"What's not my fault?"

"Nothing. Everything. I don't know."

How red his hair was beneath the warm coffeehouse lights.
He looked to her like a skinny, freckled, Scottish orphan. "You
can tell *me* a joke," she said.

"You'll hate it."

"I won't hate it."

"It's not going to be funny."

"Please?" she said.

The joke involved a horse, a carrot, and a man wearing a
cap. A third of the way through the setup, he broke character and said, "The guy in the cap is Norwegian. I forgot

to mention that." He started over and, a moment later, paused again before saying—to himself? to her?—"Is it a carrot? It's got to be a carrot, it's a horse." Looking across their small table, he could see her eyes narrowing. He sighed and—he was getting panicky now—said, "The reason the horse won't give the Norwegian a ride is that he's depressed. The *horse* is depressed, not the man." At that point he lost the thread. What in the world was he doing? He had no tolerance for comedy. He said, "How's your coffee?"

"Good. It's good."

He paid the check, and they walked out and stood on the sidewalk, which was busy with people coming and going in parkas and hats. It struck her, as she watched him standing on the dark street with his hands shoved deep into his coat pockets, that he was a decent person, a serious man, and she wanted to sleep with him, but it was too soon for that, and besides, she did not see how she could invite him to her apartment, where Susan would undoubtedly be planted on the living-room couch—the foldout couch that Jennifer slept on—watching television in a sweatshirt. Jennifer did not yet know that Christopher felt similarly thwarted, that at his place uptown on Broadway, a different Susan, home from her job, was busy smoking cigarettes, watering her overgrown plants, and talking on the telephone in a haughty, supercilious voice.

She said, "Which way are you walking?"

He said, "Which way are *you* walking?"

"You're tall," she commented as they made their way west. She said this because she was forced to hurry to keep up with him on the sidewalk. Christopher did not understand, however, that her compliment was also a plea. He did not slow his pace.

They wound up on a bench overlooking the Hudson, making out. Her mouth tasted faintly metallic to him, and he wondered whether this might indicate a problem with their chemistry. Would she be wrong for him? A wind blew in from the river, and they edged closer to each other, taking the cold as permission to mash together on the slatted bench. He worked his hand inside her coat. He didn't bother with buttons. Instead, he found passage where the coat flapped open between two closures, and felt, as his fingers burrowed under wool, the bottom of a breast. Should he push his way inside her shirt? He could hear people walking and jogging past. She kissed him harder, and, with his other hand, the hand not buried in her coat, he touched her cheek.

"Freezing hands! Ow!" She jumped up from the bench and, straightening and arranging herself, said—stating a more or less impossible proposition, he thought, considering that the city's lights, as well as those dotting New Jersey's urban hills across the Hudson, burned ceaselessly through the night— "Look how late it's getting."

Two days later, she phoned to tell him that a friend of hers was leaving town for a weekend trip, and she'd be looking in on the friend's cats. How about dinner at the friend's apartment? Would that be nice? What should she make? Did he have any food allergies that she needed to know about? "Shellfish? Chocolate? Nuts?"

"I'm fine with nuts," he said, and she told him that she'd started a new painting since meeting him, using bolder colors than she'd ever dared use in the past, and he said that he'd love to see it when it was done, and she nervously said, "I'm afraid that might be a while," and then they talked about their last couple of days. She'd done her proofreading jobs in the mornings, then painted or gone to painting class in the afternoons, whereas he had hardly strayed from his small room in his Susan's apartment, the room where he often sat late into the night, drinking, a fact he didn't let on to Jennifer. Anyway, she told him to write down her friend's address, and they rang off, and that Friday night he arrived for dinner at a studio apartment with nothing much in it but a pair of Maine coon cats and a queen-size bed stacked with pillows.

"Hello hello," he said when she opened the door.

"Careful, careful," she said, meaning: Don't let the cats out. He could see them behind her feet, angling for escape, barging about on tremendous paws matted with fur. "This is Siegfried. This is Brunhilda." With one foot, she forced aside a cat. She said, "Come in, hurry," then added, "Amy"—her friend whose apartment they were about to treat like a motel room—"is from Maine."

Quickly she closed the door.

The cats seemed a third or so larger than any house cat he'd ever seen. "You look great," he said to Jennifer, and wondered why he'd failed to bring flowers. She did look beautiful. He hadn't expected the tartan miniskirt. She'd untied her hair and let it fall, and whatever had earlier seemed hard in her appearance was tempered now. He did a turn around the tiny room. Everything—bed comforter, pillow shams and cases, headboard, the petite dresser near the front door, the phone—was white. There was even a white plastic television. The apartment was on a high floor, and an east-facing picture window overlooked the Empire State Building, lit purple and white at its tip. What holiday did purple designate? Easter? But Easter was weeks away. He sat on the edge of the mattress, then bent over with his head between his knees and stared down a big-headed animal that had wedged itself under the box spring. "Here, kitty."

"They like to play," she said.

"Which is Brunhilda?"

"That one," pointing, "the female."

Then she said, "I guess we'll have to eat on the bed." It was true. There was nowhere else to sit.

He said, "Or on the floor," though the available floor

space was not much more than a parquet walkway surrounding the bed (there was barely room to open the closet) and a kitchen area recessed along one wall. "Or in the bathroom?" he added.

She'd chosen halibut in honor of their meeting. Already they were building traditions. While he kept the cats busy with a chewed-up string dragged back and forth across the floor, she cooked the fish in one of Amy's white enamel pans, on top of Amy's white mini-stove. They squeezed onto the floor between bed and window, and balanced their plates on their knees. Paper towels were their napkins. He took a bite and said, "This is terrific."

"Is it? Do you mean that? I'm glad."

A cat crashed into his arm and he put down his fork and shoved it away.

"Don't let them bother you."

"It's not a problem. I like cats." In fact, he was allergic. He peered around the room and saw, through watery eyes, a white cosmos. He said, "I feel like I should be drinking milk."

"I think there's some in the refrigerator," she said, and he protested, "No, please, I wasn't serious," leading her to wonder if he'd been making a reference to the cats—was that it?—while he thought back over their past conversations. Had she shown a pattern of literal-mindedness? He saw her puzzlement, and felt as he always did when he allowed himself even the weakest attempt at humor. And what was with these animals that kept coming and coming, nosing around their laps and swatting at their food, so that he or Jennifer seemed always to be hoisting one and tossing it aside?

"No. Siegfried. No," Christopher scolded. His sinuses were flooding. Jennifer threw Brunhilda onto the bed and told him that she was aware that by training to paint in a manner she thought of as realistic—she was aware that, by trying to

render from life, she was covertly attacking her mother and
what she called her mother's alcoholic world view, a world
view quite accurately illustrated, she felt, in the sixties-style
abstract paintings her mother never finished, or in the ones
she finished but ruined by angrily painting past the point of
completion. "She destroys her own work," Jennifer said, and
went on to add that she, Jennifer, had recently come to feel
that she could, in her own, more representational paintings,
not only repudiate her mother but escape her; her attempt to
mirror in paint some piece of reality represented her determi-
nation to live a dignified life. That was what she believed. Or
hoped. She said, "When I study the thing I'm painting, I feel
free from not painting."

Instead of asking her, What do you mean? he said, "What
do you paint?"

"I'm one of those people standing behind an easel in Central Park."

"Really?"

"It seems quaint, but it's not. It's serious."

"No. I didn't mean . . . It's not that I . . . I," he said, and
this time—she was embarrassed for having embarrassed him—
she laughed. How could she not? Weren't couples supposed
to laugh together? Sniffling, he said, "What do I know? I'm
sorry."

"Don't apologize," she said, and whispered, consolingly,
"It's all right. It's all right." Then she confided, "I wear a beret."

"No, you don't."

"Yes, I do."

When they kissed, the metallic taste that he remembered
from the bench by the Hudson, and which he'd found himself
worrying over up in his room, was gone. Maybe it had been
neutralized by the fish. They set their plates on the floor beneath the window. He'd expected her to be nervous with

him—at what point might she leap up and end the evening with some excuse or other?—and this made him vigilant and clumsy as he unbuttoned her blouse and felt behind her back for the hooks fastening her bra. She helped him with the hooks and her shirt's bottom buttons, and she raised her arms, allowing him to unwrap her. He grabbed her hand and one of her ankles, twisting her toward him. She clutched his shirt, yanked its tail from his pants, fiercely untucking him. Behind her was the big window with its skyline view. What would it be like to come home to that?

They got up on the bed, on the pillows, and could hear Siegfried and Brunhilda snapping at the food they'd left on their plates. It was obscene, he thought, this noisy feline licking, and yet he feared that getting up and clearing the plates to the sink might be interpreted as an act of antiseptic fastidiousness, explicitly anti-sexual. He pinned her shoulders to the mattress and leaned down to bite her nipple. Though he did not yet know her body, what pressures to apply, where to linger and for how long, he managed, in spite of his worry that she would find him awkward, to hold her in a way that felt—this was something he sensed—soothing to them both. That said, it was true that she, too, passed through moments of dread. It had always been this way with her. Her heart raced, her skin got a prickly feeling, and she was forced to concentrate on breathing deeply.

Right before he pulled out and came, he looked down and caught her gazing out the window at the Empire State. He brushed her hair off her forehead, lowered his mouth to her ear, and whispered, "Are you with me, Jennifer? Are you there? Are you there, Jennifer?" This got her attention. His quiet murmuring so turned them on that it immediately became repertoire, their version of "Fuck me, fuck me."

Afterward, she told Christopher some, but not all, of the

truth of her childhood. She was afraid, though without having a clear idea why, that if she confessed too much, if she reported in full her memories of her father coming drunk into her room at night, she'd lose him. He'd sat in his underwear in a chair beside her bed, her father had, or, she said to Christopher, sometimes right on the bed, and he'd told her again and again how he loved her, and how he wished the two of them could pack their things, right this minute, and drive away together to some remote place where she'd never hear vicious fighting from the other side of the door. It would be simple. But she had to choose. Would she come with him? her father had asked her, before leaning in close and putting his arms around her neck and weeping. She would always remember the smell of his breath when he'd been drinking.

Christopher listened politely, then, sighing—his turn, once again, to show her that he could face up to his own history—confided in a whisper that he had never been anything but a goddamn disappointment to his family, and that no matter how hard he'd tried, he'd never escaped or really even understood his role as a clown, as a fool, but that he'd finally made up his mind that it didn't matter, that their opinion of him wasn't going to bother him forever. She asked him, then, whether they drank, his parents, and he, startled by this interruption, said, "Oh, you know," to which she replied, "No, I don't know. You have to tell me." And so he said, somewhat defensively, "Yes. They did. They did," then, waving his hands in the dark, went on to announce—it was as if he were making a promise—that he could handle himself in this world. And though he was not, he further acknowledged, currently employed, neither was he concerned. He had savings, in a manner of speaking, from his last and only secure position, as an associate at a law firm where he'd realized early on that he would not have the will or the desire to make partner. What point would there have been in carrying on? he asked her without really asking. He said, closing, "I'm not worried. I can find legal temp work when I need to. Hey, life's just one big process of elimination, right?" He shoved Siegfried aside, jumped up from the bed, and stood staring out at the bright city. Why was he so jittery all of a sudden? "How about a little air?" he suggested, raising the window an inch, letting in the sounds of sirens and car horns blaring far below.

Over the next months, as winter turned to spring, and spring to summer, in apartments in Manhattan and a brownstone in Brooklyn, Jennifer and Christopher developed a pattern of habitation described in rough form by the weekend at Amy's. After hauling overnight bags and specialty-shop groceries into the new house-sit, they would cook without cleaning, nose through cabinets and drawers, and fall in and out of bed, where, after screwing, they might also eat. It never took long for things to go to hell—crumbs in the sheets, ashtrays and unwashed glasses and a wine bottle or two (she liked a glass before sleep) sitting on the floor, spills drying on kitchen countertops, leftovers hardening in pans. "What a disaster," Christopher would invariably say when the time came to tidy up, and she'd answer, rolling her eyes, "Yes, but it's our disaster."

Before they made their escape, she'd scribble a note and leave gift-wrapped soap or a bottle of good olive oil (along with her leftover wine, if there was any) in a place where it would be found the minute the rightful inhabitants came through the door.

Some places worked out better than others. Karen and Peter's Little Italy walk-up facing the street was cluttered and dreary, and a tenant in a neighboring apartment had the music turned up loud, but Jennifer, intent on a good time, hauled Karen's wardrobe from the closet in search of skirts and dresses to model for Christopher. Karen had fabulous clothes,

in Jennifer's size. It wasn't long before Jennifer began pulling
out the shoe boxes as well, along with Karen's cashmere
sweaters and blazers, and parading from the bedroom in
head-to-toe outfits, while Christopher commented from his
chair on the looks that worked and those that didn't. That
was a fun night. Less enjoyable was the brownstone, where
Christopher caused basement flooding when he used paper
towels instead of toilet paper in an upstairs bathroom, clogging
a section of pipe, three stories below, that had been rusting
away for years. The owners of the house, Sam and Beth, were
away in California with their twins, Sarah and Miles, at
Sam's grandmother's memorial service. The better part of
Christopher and Jennifer's weekend was given over to negotiations with plumbers, negotiations undertaken without
consulting Sam and Beth. Finally, a man came in and sawed
away and replaced the corroded pipe, and they spent Sunday
afternoon laundering the towels they'd used to clean the floor
and the assortment of Miles's and Sarah's toys that had been
sitting in a pile beneath the leak. "That's what happens when
you buy instead of rent," Christopher announced that night
as he locked the front door behind them. He said, "Shall
we?," and they hurriedly kissed before darting off to different subways and the lives they lived separately during the
week.

Then, in May, they shut themselves up inside a modern
high-rise on Madison Avenue. For three days, they shared what
should have been a paradise of high-ceilinged rooms while
the apartment's owner, Danny, a friend of Christopher's who'd
inherited a department-store fortune, was away in Germany
buying art. He was a collector.

"Jesus," Jennifer said when they walked in. "Will you look
at this crap?" She made a clicking sound, dismissive, using
tongue against teeth. She'd stopped before a large drawing
hanging in the entryway. It was, like all the pieces displayed

on Danny's walls, abstract—a charcoal turmoil of overlapping marks, smudges, and erasures executed with such force by the artist that the paper had worn through in places.

"Do you hate it?" Christopher asked. He'd wanted her to be proud of him for scoring Danny's keys. He hadn't thought to worry about his friend's taste. She didn't answer, so he dropped their grocery bags, came up behind her, and wrapped her in a hug. Resting his chin on her shoulder, he looked at the drawing from her point of view. At first it appeared, he thought, inchoate and stagy—as if the artist had been playing with an idea about the drama in disorder. But the longer Christopher stared the more he felt compelled to see otherwise. Was that a reptile skittering across the bottom of the paper? Were those faces? He felt the muscles around his eyes relax as his gaze became less focused; outlines of faces and figures receded into the drawing's shadows, and the work acquired space and depth, interiority.

Glancing sideways, he saw that she was biting her lower lip. "How about that? It's a world," he said. She'd been thinking the same thing, though the world she saw was not his world. She saw the white walls and porch-paint gray floor inside her mother's studio, in particular the floor, its smudged arabesques and dirty footprints of paint dripped from brushes held slackly in her mother's hand, year after year, as far back as she could remember.

Why hadn't her mother protected her?

She pried Christopher's arms from her waist, stomped into the living room, and plopped down on one of the leather sofas he'd been looking forward to having sex on while listening to Danny's stereo.

"Go to hell," she said, and he flinched—was she joking? But it didn't sound like a joke.

The situation wasn't much improved in the living room. On one wall was a sculpture that looked like a complicated tricornered hat, with a high crown and a razor-edged brim. And that painting above Jennifer's head couldn't possibly be a—a what's-his-name, could it? Outside, trees were in bloom and the park was alive with insects and birds. But Danny preferred that they not open the apartment's windows. It was important to keep out dust. And, he had asked, could they please not raise the shades during the day, also for reasons having to do with conservation? Perhaps it was the drawn shades that caused Jennifer's bad mood to worsen. Christopher spent Saturday afternoon alone in the semi-darkness, flipping channels on Danny's giant television. Occasionally Jennifer called to him from the bedroom. She didn't feel like getting out of bed, even though she was sharing the room with a Richard Serra print that looked like a leaden, black sun.

"I feel sick," she told him that night when he came in and checked on her. "Do I have a fever?"

He felt her forehead. "If you do, it's not high."

"Ugh," she said.

They had another conversation about art.

"Did you paint this week?"

"I tried one day. It was windy and the stretcher blew off the easel. Twice. Anyhow, it doesn't matter. My painting is all over the place. I don't know what I'm doing."

"That can't be true."

"I don't understand color. I don't understand paint. I want things brighter. Not brighter, more alive. What am I trying to say?"

"Intense? More intense?"

She coughed. "That's part of it. I'm also searching for restraint."

"Intense restraint."

"Very funny." She coughed again.

"I didn't mean to be funny."

"I know."

He felt her forehead once more, and this time decided that she was hot. She had a temperature. He said, "I'd better get you some aspirin and a glass of water."

When he came back into the room, he sat on the bed and waited while she swallowed the pills.

"Stop staring at me."

"Sorry."

"You're making me nervous," she said. She handed him the glass. "Could you get me a drop of wine? The merlot on the counter beside the sink?"

"Is that a good idea?"

"It's Saturday night. Who cares if it's a good idea?" She held the glass for him to take. "A drop? Just a drop?"

He took the glass and went out of the room. Who drank with a fever? He made a special effort not to drink on these weekends they shared. He did not want her to see him knocking back a six-pack in the hours past midnight, as he did in secret during the week, on the nights alone—and there were other things he didn't want Jennifer to get wind of. His departure from his job hadn't come about in precisely the way he'd indicated when he'd glossed the matter on their first night together, at Amy's. Had he lied to her? He'd omitted certain specifics. She didn't need to hear about his cavalier approach to sick days or his periodic failure to bill clients, or about the humiliation he'd suffered when, one day, he'd sneaked downstairs to have a beer in the restaurant attached to the building's lobby and a partner standing at the bar had loudly upbraided him over some minor mistake, then called him a drunk. And there was something else Jennifer might not be happy knowing: He'd lately been taking walks in Central Park, hunting for her beneath the trees near Sheep Meadow and the Great Lawn. On his walks he became furtive, nervous; he imagined that if he could catch her at her easel, her brush in her hand, painting a picture of the known world, he might—he might what? Hide behind a tree and, like a trespasser hopped up on adrenaline, watch her? Call her cell phone from his and, while pretending to be nowhere near, chat?

He poured her wine and shoved the cork back into the bottle. He enjoyed a moment of pride over not having any alcohol himself. In the bedroom, he said, "Here."

She took the glass. She sat propped against pillows. She said, "A sip will help me sleep."

"Right."

"It helps before bed, you know?"

"Yes."

"Is something the matter?" she asked, because she'd heard his tone.

"No. I guess not. No." He looked at her body outlined beneath the blankets. How could he tell her what was wrong? What *was* wrong? Was it simply that he didn't care to watch her do what he did? He felt afraid for her—was that it? "It's nothing, I'm fine," he said, while she drank. But later that night he was unable to sleep. He got up and wandered into the kitchen, where he found Danny's liquor in a cabinet above the stove. He went into the living room and sat up until three drinking Scotch. His mood followed a well-worn path: Half-way through his second drink, he knew his life was good—he was a lucky man. Everything, even the glass in his hand— especially the glass in his hand, crystal, heavy-bottomed, warm to his touch—felt right to him. As he drank, his ebullience increased, and he regarded his expensive surroundings as some-how belonging to him, or, more appropriately, as a preview of what he'd surely one day have. But after another few shots his thoughts veered into a familiar loop. Who was he fooling? How would *he* ever have any of this? Why was he unable to take possession of the world's bounties? Why had he and Jen-nifer not ever gone *dancing*, for Christ's sake? What was their *plan*? They met, climbed into bed, leaped out of bed, said goodbye—was he in love? Was she? Or were they just fucking? They had so much to be thankful for, so much. They had each other.

His face was numb. He gave himself a bit more to drink, put away Danny's bottle, rinsed the glass, and groped his way down the hall to the bedroom, where he stood in his underwear beside the bed. The shades were drawn, the windows blacked out. As Christopher's eyes adjusted to the dark, he saw that each window—there were three—was haloed in a corona of light, the city's nighttime glow seeping in through the narrow chinks between glass and shade. He felt the impulse to wake Jennifer and show her the illuminated windows, as if the phenomenon represented something uniquely worth experiencing, like a solar eclipse. Three black suns hovered over her as she slept. Make that four, counting the Serra.

The following afternoon, he woke beside her. How was she feeling today? A little better, she told him. He, of course, was hungover. But that wasn't a life-or-death problem, was it? She wondered aloud if she'd given him whatever bug had bitten her, and he promised her she hadn't, then asked her—he hadn't planned this; it just came out of his mouth—if she would consider showing him her painting, the one she'd begun in the days after they met. Dry-mouthed, he added, "Don't be scared."

After that, he went ahead and joined her for drinks when they got together. Who took the lead in this new policy? It was she, after all, who didn't make much fuss over a glass of wine. Following his old rule, he waited until dinner was finished before pouring his first, so that he could have a decent amount in a short span of time without causing a sodden evening. When he drank, she drank. Sometimes she smoked. She liked to stand at a window and exhale out into the world.

When the nights got warm, she opened the window wide
and leaned on the casement.

Late in June, a heat wave hit. The daytime sky grew white
with becalmed air trapped over the city. Faint thunder could
sometimes be heard, but storms never materialized, showers
never arrived. On the evening of the solstice, Christopher
and Jennifer hauled suitcases, groceries, and her painting—
shrouded, for protection, in bubble wrap and muslin—up six
flights to Bert and Lucie's top-floor apartment. The temperature rose higher and higher as they climbed. When they reached
the landing, they stopped to rest. She recovered against a wall,
and he leaned his weight on the doorknob, then turned the
key in the lock, and they tumbled in. She went straight to the
bathroom and ran a cold tub, while he dumped ice cubes
from trays to glasses in the kitchen. He stood before the open
freezer, letting mist touch his face. He could hear her splashing in the bathroom, and he heard Bert's fish tank bubbling
in the living room. What did Bert and Lucie keep in the
freezer? Was that a bottle cap poking out from beneath two
ice-cream cartons? He pulled out the bottle of gin, unscrewed
the top, mopped his face with a dish towel, refilled the ice
trays. It was still light out. Instructions for feeding the piranha
had been left on the counter beside the sink. Christopher carried his drink down the hall and peered into the tank. He
tapped its glass wall.

"Come out, come out, wherever you are."

The bathroom door opened, closed. "I fixed you a drink!
It's in the kitchen!" he called, and heard her walking in that
direction. A moment later, he smelled cigarette smoke. He went
down the hall and saw her bent over the windowsill, her head
craned out, her back to him. She was naked and damp; the
wet ends of her hair stuck to her shoulders. She looked, he
thought, with her hair streaming back and her breasts proudly

showing, not unlike a ship's figurehead, sea-sprayed. Christopher would remember this vision—Jennifer's raised butt, framed against the building behind Bert and Lucie's, and, above that building, chimneys and water towers crowning roof after roof on the horizon—long after he'd forgotten the things they'd said in these rooms where he and she became partners.

He said, "It's too hot to eat." Dinner lay in a bag on the floor. Propped against a wall was her painting.

"No kidding." Smoke drifted from her mouth.

He leaned against the doorframe and shook his glass, clinking melting ice. "We'll have to make do with this." Was he trying to be funny? Frankly, he wasn't sure.

She shifted her weight from one foot to the other. Her feet were pink from her bath. She said, "That's fine. It's summertime," and, as if on cue, he sneezed.

"Bless you," she said, and he told her, "Something's in bloom somewhere."

She flicked ashes and came in from the window. She squeezed past him on her way to the bedroom. Dying light brightened a corner of floor and the wall beside the painting. Soon it would be dark. She returned wearing one of Lucie's see-through nighties.

He refilled their glasses.

"To home away from home."

"Cheers," she said.

In that heat, without food, they were quickly smashed. He grabbed hold of her lace nightie and, like a man in a conga line, hanging on to keep time with the leader, trotted after her down the hall. In the living room she turned on a light, and they both collapsed onto Bert and Lucie's sofa and watched the piranha tank as if it were a television set, a television broadcasting leafy weeds, luminous rocks, and bubbles, but no fish.

Was he ready to see the painting? Would he be equipped

to comment? What might he say? He was going to need a refill.

He said, "Is it worth it?"

"What?" she said. "Is what worth what?"

"Art. Painting. You know."

That made her laugh.

"The truth about you is, you're kind of a funny guy. I don't know why you fight it," she told him.

She took his hand in hers, and he turned to look at her. She pulled him close to her on the sofa. He laid his head on her lap. In a minute he would sit up and ask her if she was ready to show him the painting. She would stand up, go barefoot and tipsy to the kitchen, get it, bring it back, and, after warning, "It may not be finished, so be nice," unwrap it.

No. In a minute she would get up, and he would say, "Hey, do you mind," then hand her his glass, and she would go to the kitchen, make him a fresh drink with new ice, and bring it to him along with the painting. He would be careful, in his remarks on her work, to avoid overstating his praises. Yet he would not want her to doubt either his fundamental enthusiasm or her own promise. If the painting was accomplished, or even if not, he would find and appreciate an aspect of it—an element reflecting technical execution and artistic choice, a movement of brushstrokes indicating an intensity of gray light behind bare trees, say, since she'd begun in winter. Or she might have revised with the changing seasons, painting over winter's silvers with the pale greens and eggshell blues that signify spring. There might be a figure in the painting, a man walking quickly through the park, as he himself had done when out searching for her at her work; and maybe, if the painting showed a man, a man like him, beside a particular tree, rock, or bench, near a path that wound beside the banks of a familiar pond, he might recognize the topography and speak confidently about her handling of perspective, and about the way the light reflected off the water in precisely that way, in that place.

While he imagined his reaction to her painting, she lit another cigarette. Though he could not see the flame, he saw its image come and go, mirrored in the glass aquarium, and he sensed her hands and arms fluttering in the air above his head. He heard the match being struck.

ANOTHER MANHATTAN

They had lied to each other so many times, over so many years, that deceptions between them had become commonplace, practically repertoire. Everyone knew this about them—it wasn't news among their friends. That night, they had dinner reservations with Elliot and Susan, who were accustomed to following the shifts in attitude and tone—Kate's theatrical sighs, for instance, in reaction to Jim's mournful looks across the table at her—brought on by the strain of living in an atmosphere of worry and betrayal. It was winter, and dark, and the air in their little apartment was dry and nauseatingly warm; and yet what they needed, it seemed to Jim, was not to flee their home for another night of exciting conversational pauses and sly four-way flirting. They needed to sit down together, no matter how stuffy it got in the living room, no matter how loudly the radiators hissed and banged, and take turns speaking their minds. They had to talk. But first he would stop at the florist's on his way home from the outpatient clinic. If he walked through the door carrying a bouquet, there was a chance that Kate might smile.

There was a chance also that it wouldn't look awkward or strange when, at the end of the evening—he didn't really be-lieve that he and Kate would be staying in—he paired with

Susan for the walk through the cold, from the restaurant to
Elliot's car. It might look, in other words, as if he were not
bothered by Kate's whispering to another man. (She had a
way, with Elliot, of bowing her head and mumbling furiously
through the strands of hair that fell across the side of her face,
so that, in order to make out her words, Elliot was forced to
stoop and lean into the fog of her breath.) Jim's own affair, his
affair with Susan, had been over for almost five months, long
enough, he thought, as he approached the florist's on the corner
by his and Kate's building, for him to begin experimenting—
later that same night, if the mood was right—with innocently
putting his arm around Susan's shoulder while she and he and
Kate and Elliot walked in two sets of two toward the parking
garage.

Of course, he wanted to be careful not to punish Kate, or
at least not to seem to punish her, for her success in adultery.
Elliot made her laugh—in a sweet way. Anyone meeting them
for the first time would think they were a new couple.

It was wrong to hate her.

He'd arrived at the florist's. Inside, he went straight over
to the roses in their refrigerated case. Though it was a cold
day, cold and very windy, and he'd come in chilled, the short
walk across the heated space warmed him, and he could feel
the frigid air hit him in the face when he yanked open the glass
door. He leaned in and peered at the flowers. He asked the
girl, "Do you have yellow roses that haven't already bloomed
and, you know, opened?"

Yellow roses, signifying friendship more than eros, seemed
right, given the complex potentials of the evening.

"We only have these."

"They're pretty, but they're not going to last."

She was pretty as well, the girl showing him roses. Had he
seen her in here before and somehow not noticed? How old
was she? Should he risk looking into her eyes? Was she wearing

a ring? What about her ass? And what had he said to her just now? Blooming and opening meant the same thing in relation to flowers. He'd become inarticulate in her presence.

Kate, in the meantime, was upstairs in the apartment, talking on the phone to Elliot. The call had gone on for more than five hours. Kate had had to use all available phones: her cell phone and, before the cell, the apartment's two cheap cordless handsets, one in the kitchen and one in the bedroom. "Can you hear beeping? I've got to switch phones. Hang on," she'd exclaimed when the kitchen phone's battery began dying. Carrying that phone (her first of the call), she'd gone into the bedroom, picked up its brother from the night table, and said, into this new phone, "Are you there? Can you hear me? Hold on while I hang up the other phone," after which she'd taken both phones to the kitchen and dropped the dead one into its cradle on the wall. A small cabinet door beside this phone opened onto a narrow and dark airshaft that had once housed a dumbwaiter. Kate opened and closed this empty cabinet several times while explaining, on the bedroom phone, why Elliot's being married and her being married shouldn't necessarily be considered something they had in common. That they were both childless could stand as an area of emotional parity, she felt, considering the fact that they both remained unsure as to whether to have children, while their spouses frequently made it clear that, in their opinions— Susan's specifically regarding Elliot, Jim's specifically regarding Kate, and neither Susan nor Jim meaning to suggest a marital reconfiguration—they'd make "a great dad" or "a great mom."

Elliot interrupted: "Don't you get tired of hearing that?"

"It's beside the point," Kate answered, and went on, "Oh, Elliot, why is talking to you so damn fucking difficult?"

"Do you need an answer?"

"You know me, always curious." How stupid was that?

She'd been trying, not for the first time, to lovingly make clear to Elliot why she could no longer sleep with him. During the first hours of the conversation she'd been able to control the impulse to bait and flirt. But the business of swapping phones, the walking from room to room in the stuffy apartment, had, as it were, weakened her. It was as if, in losing that first phone, she'd lost a line of defense, however symbolic, against Elliot's desire. Or maybe, she thought as she stood in the kitchen, opening and closing the dumbwaiter door with one hand, the necessary act of sacrificing one phone for another could be read as a veiled enactment of the sort of ambivalence required for alternating between lovers in the first place. Or was that too absurd?

"Say that once more. I didn't hear what you were saying," she said to Elliot. The heating pipes banged; day was turning to dusk. She listened to the hiss of steam escaping from the radiator beneath the kitchen window. Elliot began again, "I was saying that I sometimes think that you think that because I'm a psychiatrist I can automatically see all the different sides of a situation. But I'm not that kind of psychiatrist."

"Please don't talk to me like I'm one of your postdocs," she said, and he took a long breath.

He said, "Kate, we're involved with each other, Kate."

"Jim's your friend."

"And so are you my friend."

"Your wife is my friend, too." She continued, "Fuck, I hate this. Now *this* motherfucking phone is beeping. Hold on. Elliot, can you hold on?" She swapped the bedroom phone for the insufficiently charged kitchen phone, went with that phone back into the bedroom, and sat on the edge of the bed.

"Kate, why are you bringing up Susan? I need to know what your point is. We agreed that we weren't going to talk about Susan. So where are you going with this? Kate? Are you there?"

He waited.

"Will you talk to me? Please, don't do this. Don't do this, Kate. All right, fuck this, fuck this, fuck—"

His phone was beeping. It wasn't the battery. It was another call. He said, "Kate, hang on a minute. Hang on, Kate."

He took the call. "Hello?"

"It's me," she said, and then told him in a miserable voice that both her home phones were dead, and that she was on her cell phone and just wanted to say that she didn't much enjoy dishonesty.

"You'll have to speak up," he said.

"Can you hear me? Tell me when the signal is clear." She pressed the cell phone against her ear and walked from the bedroom to the living room, then into the kitchen, then straight down the hall, passing the tiny second bathroom, with the broken, unusable toilet, to the apartment's miniature front foyer.

"Here?" she said. "Here?"

"I'm losing you," he said. And so she retraced her route, winding up back in the living room, where she turned on a lamp. The sky was dark. Everywhere on the city's horizon she saw other people's lit windows. Once again, Elliot had bullied her—or she'd *let* him bully her—into leaving open the question of their affair. What was the use in arguing, anyway? Jim would come home any minute, and, a little later, the two of them would go out and meet Elliot and Susan for dinner. How crazy was that? She still had to shower and dress. She conceded to Elliot, "All right, I'll think about it."

"Tomorrow, then?" Elliot said, and added, "I knew you'd come to your senses." He joked that if he didn't get out of his office in the next few minutes he'd be forced to show up at the restaurant in his white coat. They said goodbye, and she put down the phone and wept for a quarter of an hour.

Downstairs at the florist's, Jim's bouquet for Kate was

growing and growing. It featured not only yellow roses but red and pink solitaires, along with sprigs of heather, freesia, and alstroemeria; green and white calla lilies; blue irises; mums; and some other things the girl had plucked from buckets and waved in the air for him to see and approve. "What else? What does she like?" she'd asked him, as she leaned into the refrigerator and reached for more.

"That looks so nice. I think she'll like just what you like," he said, and wondered whether it was okay for him to have said it. Was it provocative? There were no other customers in the shop. Staying close but keeping his distance, he followed the girl from one display case to another. He might as well have been buying lingerie, he felt; and, in fact, it seemed to him that the bouquet was somehow intended for the girl, as much as for Kate, who would've been, well, not exactly mortified to know that her husband was downstairs using a shopgirl as a proxy to get himself worked up for sex later that night.

"Baby's breath," the girl said to him.

"Excuse me?"

"I love baby's breath."

"In that case, we'll have to have a bunch," Jim said.

"Good."

She turned away, laid the unfinished bouquet on its side on the countertop beside the cash register, and, with her back to him, said, "We have a *lot* to work with here." She glanced back over her shoulder (did she want him to come closer?), then, quickly—what a great flirt, he thought—turned away again and set to work breaking down the bouquet and separating the flowers into groups, a variegated series of stacks that she arranged not by color or type (except in the case of the combined red, pink, and yellow roses) but, as became clear, by stem length. When she had her piles, she picked up clippers.

"This will take a minute," she said.

He watched her snip the stems. He said, "Take your time."

But there was a problem: What were these flowers going to cost? The bouquet as she assembled it—as it came to *be*, in her hands—was broader and taller by far than what he'd come into the florist's wanting. It was less a bouquet than a proper arrangement, a centerpiece, thanks in part to the leafy green branches the girl stuffed between blossoms, and the pale white baby's breath, which she didn't so much layer as clump into the globular mass.

"Can we take some out?" he asked, and wished he hadn't. What kind of man courts a woman by letting her make an enormous bouquet for his wife, then asks her to pare back?

"What would you like me to take out?" the girl asked. Was she annoyed? She had her back to him. Did she think less of him? Did she think he was a cheap bastard who cheats on his wife?

"It's just that I was hoping to use a particular Arts and Crafts vase on the mantel, which, in my opinion, these would look lovely in," he elaborately lied. (Actually, there was a vase on the mantel—but so what?) He went on, "What I mean to say is that the vase I have in mind isn't very big."

Did he need excuses? Did he need to bring up his home life?

He went into reverse. "Come to think of it, never mind about that vase on the mantel. It would be a shame to wreck such a nice bouquet."

"I'm not going to wreck anything."

Was she scolding him? Were things heating up between them? He waited for her next move.

"I can give you a bigger vase," she proposed, finally.

He held his breath. She had to be at least twenty years younger than he. But it wasn't their age difference, nor the fact that he was married, that made him feel uncertain of himself.

The problem was his thought process: The lithium he was taking in small doses brought a slower speed to reality. It was the lithium or the antidepressant cocktail or all of it in concert. At times, when he spoke, he felt as if a kind of mental wind were blowing his thoughts back at him, forcing him to self-consciously order his syntax as he pushed words out.

"I just got—I just got out of the hospital!" he blurted.

He watched her as she turned to face him; in her hands she held white lilies and a red satin bow, and her eyes looked left, right, left.

"I shouldn't've said that! Forget I said that! I didn't mean to say that! Give me the vase. I want a vase."

"Oh!" she said, as if startled to realize that she was still clutching pieces of the bouquet. "Let me run in the back and get one."

While Jim and the girl sorted themselves out downstairs, Kate was marching around the apartment in her red heels, shoving things into her purse and looking in the usual places for her keys. She had to flee before Jim walked in. She could phone him from the street and tell him that she'd meet him at the restaurant. Going from Elliot to Jim to Elliot *and* Jim *and* Susan without a break was bullshit. But, seriously, where was she going to go? It was too cold out to sit on a bench. The bar next door to the restaurant was bleak and depressing, an old men's dive, and the bar inside the restaurant would be a mob scene of people pushing for tables. She could stand idly flipping through magazines at the newsstand across Broadway, but that would mean accommodating the line of men squeezing past her to look at porn at the rear of the store. She slammed the apartment door behind her and started down the five flights of stairs. Too often in winter she failed to leave the apartment before sunset. It worked hell on her mood.

Outside, the wind was blowing hard. She wasn't wearing

a hat. She tightened her scarf around her neck, tugged up her coat collar, lowered her head, and walked toward Broadway with her fists punched down into her pockets and her purse clinched under her arm. If only it would snow. But when did it ever snow anymore? Hat or no hat, she wouldn't have minded a few snowflakes swirling down through the city light to settle on her head. When she'd been a girl, snow had lain on the ground all winter. That was what she remembered. Of course, she was thinking of the farm, of New England, not New York. So what was her point? These days, it rarely snowed the way it had back in the years before her parents died. The snowfalls she remembered from her childhood seemed lost to time and, she supposed, the changing climate.

She hurried along as quickly as she could in her high heels. At Broadway, she turned uptown and passed the florist's, where the pretty shop assistant had just come out from the back with the flowers—flowers for *her*, for Kate—in their vase.

"Here we are," the girl announced to Jim. She extended her arms and held the flowers out in front of her, presenting them. Before he could move to take them from her, however—it was the medication, warping his mind and delaying his reaction—she heaved the arrangement onto the counter and explained that she'd had to search high and low for an extra-heavy vase, one that was not only broad enough but also deep enough to properly anchor the bouquet.

Jim and the girl admired her creation. With its stalks vertical and free to fan out or droop down, the bouquet's real immensity became apparent. Roses with their thorns stuck out everywhere, and the lilies, whose columnar stalks the girl had bunched at the center, shot up through the top of the bouquet like, like, like—like insane trees towering above some insane world, he thought. He was light-headed when he spoke. "I love the way you've used ribbons and bows to tie the blossoms into clusters. It looks like a bouquet made of little bouquets!

There's so much to see. I can smell the lilies. Don't you want to inhale that scent? Do you know the painter Fragonard? Do you know Boucher? Look at Boucher's flowers. They're practically obscene. There might be a Boucher hanging at the Frick."

He went for it. "Do you like museums?"

"When I have time."

"I could show you the Frick." He grinned widely and shrugged his shoulders and tipped his head, and she mirrored him, shrugging her own shoulders and making a funny face.

"You're very good at what you do," he added, and she said, "Thank you," then asked him, "How would you like to pay?"

He tried to imagine what he'd be forced to spend. Whatever the amount, it would be too great. The bills from his recent hospitalizations were mainly covered by Kate's insurance—the policy was hers; they'd gone ahead and got married in order for him to take advantage of it during this protracted (Kate's word, sometimes used sarcastically) time of crisis in his life—but there were nevertheless many outstanding fees, brand-new bills arriving every other week, plus the only partly reimbursable expense of the aftercare program he attended across town, on the Upper East Side.

"Let's charge it." He handed the girl his debit card.

She swiped the card. "It's not going through," she said. After passing the card through the machine a second time, she apologized. "This doesn't automatically mean that there's a problem with the account," she said. "You'll have to contact your bank. Would you like to try another account?"

"I don't have another. Tell me the total?"

"Three hundred and forty-one dollars and sixty cents."

His anxiety spiked and he took a breath. How could a bouquet of flowers be that much?

He put his hand in his pocket and felt around for cash, but what was the point?

"Hold on a minute," he said.

What to do, what to do? He was going to have to call his wife. Was he going to have to call her? He was going to have to call her. He took out his phone and dialed—in that moment he was glad that he had his meds on board—and right away Kate picked up and hollered, "Where *are* you? I'm at the restaurant with Susan! Elliot is out parking the car. Did you go to your *therapy*?"

"Could you not shout, Kate?"

"It's goddamn packed in here!"

"I need to talk to you, privately," he said, and turned away from the shopgirl. But there was no way, in the small space, to keep the girl from overhearing, so he put his hand over the phone, leaned toward her, and whispered, "I'll be right back," then stepped out of the shop, stood on the sidewalk in the freezing wind, and slowly, deliberately humiliated himself, saying to Kate, "I stopped on my way home and bought you flowers, but the bank account isn't cooperating with my card for some reason and now I'm stuck at the florist's because I don't have enough cash on me, and I think the problem is simply that—shit, I don't know what the problem is, I must not have kept my eye on the balance, and it's possible that we're overdrawn. I know we've talked about this. But it's not a serious problem, I promise."

"Oh, Jim. Are you *spending*? How much have you *spent*?" Kate cried, and he winced.

He said, "Is Susan there?"

"Do you not hear a word I say? She's right here! We're drinking Manhattans. Are you coming? We're waiting for you. Why do you want to talk to Susan? Jim, are you spending our money?"

"I don't want to talk to Susan. I'd just prefer that this conversation be private between the two of us."

"Please, Jim, as if everyone we know doesn't already know everything there is to know?"

"I'm not—I am not spending our money."

"You're agitated."

"Why are you diagnosing me? I'm not agitated. I wanted to surprise you with flowers. But clearly it was just another of my many mistakes. I'll think twice next time. Everything I do is unwanted."

"Stop it," Kate said to him then.

Through the phone he could hear sounds from the restaurant bar, voices and other noises in the after-work crush. Then the wind came up, and the only sound he heard was the phone's own static. The wind died, and Kate's voice was saying, "Elliot is here now, and Lorenzo is clearing us a table. Let me talk to someone about the flowers."

In this way he was forced to trudge back into the shop, hold the phone out, and say to the girl, "She wants to talk to you."

The girl hesitated, then reached out and let him pass the phone into her hand.

"Hello?" she said into his phone.

He retreated to a corner of the store. Joking aside, he didn't care to loiter about, smelling the flowers, while the girl wrote down his wife's American Express number. He would never learn the girl's name, not now, Kate would see to that, he told himself as he peered out from his hiding place behind a leafy potted tree. He saw the shop's buckets of flowers and the refrigerators in a row, and the door leading to the back, but where was the girl? He heard her laugh in response to some remark Kate must've made, and realized that she was standing behind the bouquet. "Oh, don't I just know that about men and their important purchases!" she exclaimed.

What was Kate saying to her? Was he being made fun of? Was she calling him bipolar?

He had a problem with anxiety and suicidality, and, as Kate had reminded him in their conversation a moment earlier, everyone knew about his previous autumn's sojourns on the Fifty-ninth Street Bridge and his games of chicken—no, not games, not at all, really—on the fire escape outside their bedroom window.

He didn't want to think about any of that. Yet it was the reason he was now crouched behind a ficus, eavesdropping while a girl he wanted to fuck got treated to an earful of Kate—on *his* phone! And what was the big problem, anyway, if a handful of times on his way home from day care, as he sometimes called his ongoing treatment, he'd got excited about life and jumped off the crosstown bus at Fifth Avenue and run into Bergdorf Goodman and ridden the elevator to the second floor and tried on clothes until closing? Was that unhealthy? His doctors didn't think he was manic-depressive; in fact, they'd ruled it out. Kate had been reading the clinical literature, though, and felt autodidactically certain that the Payne Whitney professionals were minimizing something in plain sight: His death-trip history, considered alongside the "conspicuous" spending on coats, ties, shirts, and shoes, represented, at the least, she thought, a mixed-state depression. "Why don't they have you on olanzapine?" she'd got in the habit of asking him. He begged her not to interfere with his treatment, and suggested—thinking of her father's death and the forfeiture of the family farm in Massachusetts, when she was a teenager— that her consuming anxiety about bankruptcy, her emphasis on this as a potentially mortal trauma, might have less to do with his new handmade suits than with the ways in which his almost dying had reactivated an old mourning in her.

He peered from behind the ficus. He was wearing a ridiculous cashmere overcoat, and his suit today was a medium-gray flannel herringbone. It featured, on the jacket, minimal shoulder padding, dual vents, and a graceful, three-rolled-to-two-button stance (his current favorite lapel style), and, on the pants, single reverse pleats and one-and-a-quarter-inch-cuffed trouser legs. Why would a man ever not cuff his trousers? He kept a single jacket-sleeve button open on the left, another open on the right. He didn't look like blown credit. Did he?

Kate was going to kill him. She was mad enough to kill him. That was a fact. What was he doing, charging expensive flowers for no reason on an average night in the middle of the week when they were already committed to a crippling tab—it was sure to be a huge bar bill, by evening's close—for dinner with Elliot and Susan? But, Kate thought, as she sat with their friends, waiting for him at a tiny table near the back of the restaurant, this was how it went with her husband: He made the gestures; she absorbed the costs. "How awful this all is," she sighed. She was on the phone to the girl at the florist's. Kate hadn't meant to be audible, not to the girl, and certainly not to Elliot, who would take her vexation over Jim as a cue to call her up the next day and argue for more afternoons at the hotel.

She'd been going once or sometimes twice a week to the Upper East Side to meet Elliot at the Lowell Hotel, on Sixty-third Street between Madison and Park. She rode the bus. Typically, she arrived first. She got the room key, went up, and showered; if Elliot was delayed at the lab and the day was growing dark, she might unlock the minibar and make a Man-hattan or an approximation of a Manhattan, then recline naked by the window and look north toward the East Nineties, Car-negie Hill, where her mother, an only child, like Kate, had lived before marrying her father and moving to the farm.

Manhattans had been her mother's drink. Unlike her mother, Kate tried to keep herself to three an evening. At

Lorenzo's that night, she was ahead of pace, finishing her second before having eaten a bite. She held her glass in one hand and her phone in the other, listening hard through the restaurant noise as the girl at the florist's recited back her AmEx number. Elliot sat quietly beside her. He had his arms crossed, and his chair pushed back at an angle to make room for his legs. Susan had got up from the table; she'd announced to Kate—sounding well on the way to being tight—"Kate, you're my best friend, but I don't know how you drink such a strong drink." To Kate and Elliot together, she'd added, "Will you two do me a big giant favor? Will you snag Lorenzo and ask him to bring me a Cosmo?"

"Don't utter a word to me about my husband," Kate warned Elliot, once Susan had gone to the bathroom.

Into the phone, to the girl, she said, "I'm sorry, I didn't mean you. I was talking to somebody else."

Meanwhile, in the women's room, Susan was on her own phone, calling Jim's number from a stall.

It was the girl who answered, of course.

"Hello, can you hold?" the girl said. The line went briefly dead. After a pause, the girl came back and said, "May I ask who is calling?"

"May I ask who's answering?"

"Hold, please."

"Sir?" the girl called out to Jim. She looked this way and that for him. Where had he gone? The shop closed at eight. It was nearly closing time. "A woman is calling you!"

"I'm here! I'm right here!" he answered from behind his tree.

"He'll be with you in one second," he heard her promise into the phone. After that, there was a pause, before, in a businesslike tone, the girl resumed with Kate. "I'm sorry to have to ask you this again. Would you mind verifying the last five digits and the expiration date?"

Back when he was in the hospital—in the past six months, there had been three emergency-room visits and two locked-ward admissions—he had spent day after day lying on a mattress, crying. His doctors (along with the psychiatric nurses and the social workers who led the daily therapy groups) had encouraged him to uncurl himself from the fetal position and try, at least try, to watch television or play a board game with the other patients, but this had mostly proved too great a challenge. There had been times when, walking to or from the bathroom or the water fountain or the patients' common room, or standing in line to receive his medications at the nurses' station, or even simply sitting upright on the table in the examining room, he'd had the strong sensation that the air through which he moved was gathering around him and becoming—really, no word was sufficient to name it— substantive. Its weight pressed in on him. This hurt, it hurt terribly, yet when he tried to locate the source of the pain he could not: It came, as he knew, only from himself. On the mattress, shattered and sobbing over Kate and their messed-up love, he'd lain crushed.

"Sir?"

The girl's voice seemed to echo through the shop. He peeked up. When had she come out from behind the bouquet? He could see her standing on the other side of the tree. She was looking at him through the leaves.

"Are you all right, sir?"

"I maybe—I need a minute." His mouth was dry and his heart was beating fast. That could be his meds.

"There's someone who wants to talk to you. Do you think you can take the call? Would you like to try?" She held his phone out with one hand, reaching toward him through the branches.

He had to reach into the tree to meet her hand. He was sweating.

"Hello?" he said into the phone.

"What the hell, Jim?" Susan said to him from the women's-room toilet at Lorenzo's.

"Susan, how are you?" he said.

"I've been better."

"I'm sorry."

"We're all here, Jim. We're waiting and waiting for you."

"I'm doing my best to get there. Have you ordered yet? What are the specials? What looks good?"

"Kate is beside herself. She says the two of you are bank-rupt. She says you've spent all the money."

"I haven't."

"Don't lie to me, Jim. Please, don't lie to me." She was sniffling, beginning to weep, lightly.

"Stop crying, stop crying, baby," he whispered into the phone. Then he laid his hand over the receiver and said to the girl, who was still peering down at him through the leaves of the tree, "You'll have to excuse me one more time." With a powerful effort of will, he stood upright and came out from behind the ficus. He didn't dare look at the girl, but he heard her telling him, as he pushed painfully past her toward the door, that it looked like his wife's American Express card wasn't working, either—and was there any way for him to pay for the flowers?

He waved his hand, motioning that he'd return. He stepped out into the cold on Broadway. He pulled up his overcoat's shawl collar. The door to the florist's closed behind him.

Back at their table for four, Kate and Elliot had hit a snag.

"Let me talk to him," Elliot said. He had his elbows on the table. He'd drunk almost none of his Scotch.

"That's not a good idea."

"Give me your phone." He held out his hand.

"I'm on hold."

"Kate," he said.

"Leave me alone."

"As you wish," he said, leaning back in his chair, and she burst out at him, "How can you act like this? You're a doctor. How can you be so unfeeling?"

He said, "What does my being a doctor have to do with my feelings?" (She rolled her eyes at this, but he didn't appear to notice.) He went on, "I may be a doctor, but I'm not your husband's doctor."

"His name is Jim, remember?"

"I think you're drunk. That's what I think."

He got up from the table, patted his pockets—checking for his own phone—and said, "Goddamn it, I do research. I don't treat patients. He has excellent doctors. I'll call him myself."

When he'd gone and Kate was alone, Lorenzo arrived with Susan's Cosmopolitan.

"Everybody has gone away and left you," Lorenzo said, and Kate chirped back, "Everybody's gone!"

"Let me bring you another Manhattan." Lorenzo placed Susan's cocktail on the table and picked up Kate's empty glass. Kate managed a little smile. She held her phone to her ear. "Jim? Jim, are you there?" she whispered.

Six blocks downtown, Jim was on the line to Susan. "I'm here, I'm here with you, baby," he assured her. In fact, he wasn't thinking of sleeping with her again. Oh, he'd loved sleeping with Susan—that wasn't the problem. But that evening his body was compressing: The weight of the air was on him, flattening his libido and his trust in humankind.

"Susan," he said. "Susan."

"What is it?" she said. Her voice filled the stall. "What is happening? Is it happening? Is it happening to you now? I'm scared. What do I *do*?"

"Susan," he said. "Susan."

He explained to her that in a few minutes he was going to

calmly walk back inside the florist's and steal a mysterious and beautiful bouquet that he and an angel had made for Kate. He'd helped the angel, he pointed out. He was feeling honest. He acknowledged to Susan that he was speaking metaphorically when it came to angels—in order to seem aboveboard and keep her trust. He needed her to be cool when he entered the restaurant, he told her. Then he ended the call and switched over to Kate.

"I'm coming," he said.

"I'm glad," she said.

"I love you," he said.

"I love you, I love you," she said. She was alone at their table.

She said, "Have you talked to Elliot?"

He said, "I haven't heard from him."

Elliot, in the meantime, had been unable to get through, Jim's phone lines having been taken up by both their wives. He'd left two messages already, one saying, "Jim, call me, all right?"; the other, "Jim, will you call me?" His third attempt got through, but Jim didn't answer. He heard the beeping, plucked the phone away from his ear, glanced at it, saw who was calling, and said, to Kate, "It's him. There is no way that I want to speak to him right now."

"I understand," she said. Then she said, "Just get here, dear, and have dinner with us. We all need food. We need to eat."

He said, "Has he taken care with you, since I've been gone?"

"Gone?" she said.

"I don't know how else to put it."

She asked, "Will you stay where you are, until people come?"

"Don't send an ambulance," he said to her.

He put his phone in his pocket. He turned and faced the door to the flower shop. A few people swept past him on the windy avenue—or so it seemed; his thoughts were with the pain beneath his temple. He wanted to put it out. He could imagine different ways to do this. This was how it was when his mind turned to high open windows or unlocked rooftop fire doors or breaks in the chain-link fences lining bridge walkways.

He took a step forward. The door was made partly of glass, and he could see into the shop. It occurred to him that it would be easy to break the window with his fist and deliberately cut up the veins in his arms. Instead, he put his hand on the doorframe and pushed. He stuck his head inside. He was acting guiltily, though he knew there was no reason to, not at the florist's—he hadn't done anything yet. Still, he snuck in, ashamed.

The girl was nowhere in sight. The bouquet looked bigger than it had the last time he'd sized it up. How would he manage to get it up Broadway in his trembling hands? Beside it on the table—careful, he had to be careful—were the girl's pruning shears, as well as regular scissors and a small sharp knife.

He told himself to let those things lie.

Uptown at the restaurant, Lorenzo brought Kate her drink. She asked for bread, and apologized to him for taking so long to order dinner. "We'll all be here together soon," she sighed.

She was right about that. Elliot had given up trying to reach Jim, and the cold had driven him back inside. He was threading his way down the aisle to their table. Susan, too, would return, as soon as she had peed. Pride had made her unable to while on the phone.

And that left Jim, who had no desire to become a thief. Might he, instead, offer something in barter for the flowers? His wristwatch wasn't worth much. His overcoat was brandnew, and cost well more than the watch and the bouquet combined. He decided to leave an IOU, promising to come back another day with money, or if not with actual money, then with a clear idea of when one or another of his or his wife's credit cards might again be active and usable.

But when he tried to hold a pen in his hand, he could not; and when he tried to focus his eyes on the piece of paper lying beside the cash register—it was the scrap of a receipt on which the girl had penciled Kate's American Express information—he found that his mind was frantic. This was his disorder. This was the descent. He crumpled the receipt and shoved it into his pocket. He reached for the bouquet. The girl had put water in the vase.

Had you been walking downtown on Broadway that February night at a little past eight, you might have seen a man hurrying toward you with a great concrescence of blooms. You might have noticed that he did not even pause for traffic signals, but charged across streets against the lights; and so you might rightly have supposed that he could not see through the flowers that he held (doing what he could to keep clear of thorns) at arm's length before him. Whenever a siren sounded in the distance—and, once, beating helicopter blades in the night sky caused him to sprint up a side street—he dropped into a furtive, crouching gait. His balance was off; he was paranoid about police. Windblown flowers lashed at his head. Seen from a distance, he might have brought to mind an old, out-of-favor stereotype: the savage in a headdress. But as he came closer, you would have noticed his European clothes, his stylish haircut; and you might have asked yourself, "What's wrong with that man?"

Had you stepped to the side as he hurtled past, tightened your scarf securely around your neck, and continued on your way, you might next have encountered a young woman on a street corner, distraught and coatless. "Did you happen to see a man carrying a bouquet of flowers?" she might have asked in a startled voice, and you would have looked away from her bare, pale legs, pointed upwind, and told her, "He went that way." By then, the first snowflakes would have been swirling through the caverns between the apartment buildings, down onto the thoroughfare.

Jim looked up and saw the snow on his way into Lorenzo's. For an instant, he took it as an omen—of what, though? He pulled hard on the restaurant door, forcing it open, and stumbled with his tattered flowers into the dark realm between the door and the velvet drapes that had been hung to keep the cold from sweeping in over diners at the front of the room.

He parted the curtains. "Pardon me," he said to the people seated near the entrance. Long- and short-stemmed flowers alike had snagged on the drapes. Now a waiter approached— and here came Lorenzo, too, calling, in his soft, ristoratore's voice, "*Ciao*, James. *Ciao*. I cannot call you Jim, you know."

"Lorenzo, *ciao*," Jim said. The waiter was busy tugging on the curtains. Lorenzo lent a hand. "This way, try this way," Lorenzo instructed. Jim spun left then right, enshrouding himself—and the bouquet—within the folds of drapery fabric. There followed a flurry of petals. The rose thorns came loose; the bouquet's topmost stems sprung free. He tumbled out into the room.

"I'm good, I'm fine," he said, nodding reassuringly (he hoped) to Lorenzo, the waiter, the people who'd turned in their seats to stare.

"What has happened to you, James?" Lorenzo pulled his white silk pocket square from his breast pocket and reached around the yellow and pink and blue and white flowers to dab at Jim's forehead.

"I ran all the way here," Jim said.

"You're bleeding," Lorenzo told him. Jim saw the blood spotting Lorenzo's handkerchief.

Lorenzo said, "You have a lot of scratches. You look like

you've been in a fight with some squirrels or something." He laughed, nicely.

"I've—I have been fighting, Lorenzo. Not with squirrels. Roses," Jim specified, and Lorenzo said, "Ah, of course. Let me take them."

He spoke to the waiter. "Paul, will you please take these from James?" To Jim, he added, "We will bring them to your table."

"No, no," Jim said. He explained to Lorenzo that the flowers were a gift for Kate, and that he needed to present them himself. This was crucial, he told Lorenzo. He clutched the vase. His pants were wet from water that had sloshed over the rim. Water stained his shoes. He could see tiny snags marking the sleeves of his overcoat and the front of his suit. How frustrating, after having labored so hard to avoid the thorns. His clothes would have to go to a reweaver, he thought. Then his thinking disintegrated into bitter resignation. Everything he touched was ruined. The flowers were almost destroyed.

Nonetheless, he bore them down the aisle. Here and there, people ducked forward in their chairs, or to the side, letting him through. As he progressed toward the back, the room quieted. People put down their silverware, their wineglasses; Jim felt eyes watching him.

"Eat! Live while you can!" he wanted to proclaim to the crowd. But what did he have to teach anyone? He was a thief, a common criminal—worse. He'd stolen a bouquet to give to the love of his life.

When she saw him, she was filled with happiness. She'd had a lot to drink—but, well, it wasn't that alone.

"Kate," he said. She stood, and he lurched toward her. Elliot and Susan stood as well. They flanked Kate, who came out from between them—not unlike Jim, she was unsteady on her feet—saying, "I'm sorry, excuse me," as she tacked her way through the sea of tables.

They met near the bathrooms. The bar was to their right. Kate raised her open hands to wipe the blood from his face. Blood had run down his neck, and stained the collar of his shirt. "These are for you," he told her.

She was quietly crying, whispering, "They're beautiful, beautiful." Then her crying began in force, and she wailed, "You made it, oh, you *made* it, we were all so scared, and I felt so lost."

"I'm here," he said, and his own tears started. He wanted to tell her that everything would be better, that *he* would be better, that one day soon he would work again, and start paying some bills, and take the burden off her shoulders; that they would be able, at last, to leave the little apartment with the busted plumbing. He wanted to tell her how much he needed her.

But he could see, out of the corner of his eye, his horrid reflection in the mirror behind the bar. He looked down at Kate's hands, the blood smeared across her palms. And he saw the restaurant-goers and the waiters and waitresses and busboys, who, not knowing what to make of the bleeding and the crying and the broken lilies arcing over Jim's and Kate's heads like some insane wedding canopy, had come from the kitchen or the bar to stand mutely around them. The pain in his body grew, and the words that spilled out of him were not words of love. Or they were. He spoke to his wife, as he spoke to the people gathered.

"Don't you see, Kate? Don't you *see*? It's time for me to go. I can't do this anymore. I have no place here. I don't belong. I hurt so. You can live and be happy. That will never be true for me."

"No, no, baby," she wept at him.

Someone touched his arm. It was Elliot, who'd come up behind him. He said to Jim, "Let's get in the car."

Lorenzo was there, too. Kate said to Jim, "Honey, let Lorenzo take the flowers. Just for now," and he did.

A moment later, Lorenzo came back with a wet cloth. Kate used it to wipe her eyes and to clean Jim's face and her hands. She tied the belt around his overcoat. She said, "There."

They went out of the restaurant, the four of them. Susan let Jim lean on her, and Elliot steadied Kate. On the way out the door, they heard Lorenzo, behind them, telling his patrons, "Everything is all right. Our friend has had a bad time. Please, let me buy everyone a drink."

On Broadway, the wind had died, and the air seemed to have warmed. They walked out into new snow. And, wouldn't you know, Jim did wrap his arm around Susan's shoulders, and Elliot ducked down close to Kate, listening to her mumble whatever it was she had to say to him.

At the garage, Jim and Kate got into the backseat of Elliot's car. Susan sat beside Elliot. Elliot started the engine, turned on the headlights and the windshield wipers. *Thump, thump, thump.* He steered east. During the trip, Jim took his belt from around his waist. He gave Kate his scarf and his phone and his keys and all his money, which amounted to about thirty dollars.

Later, she would get on her knees on the emergency-room floor and extract the laces from his shoes. A nurse would come, then another, and a doctor promising sleeping pills.

By that time, after midnight, Elliot and Susan would have driven up the FDR Drive and out of Manhattan, through the Bronx, and into Westchester County.

"You can go home now, if you'd like," the doctor said to Kate. "We won't let anything happen to him."

He gave Kate a plastic garbage bag, into which she put

Jim's overcoat and his suit jacket. She would use the last of his money for her crosstown taxi, and for milk and cereal at the Korean market near the apartment.

In the deep of the night, they came for him. A male nurse helped him into a wheelchair, and then pushed him through the white labyrinth of hallways and waited for the elevator.

Margaret, one of the night nurses, met him on the ward. She said, "Hello, Mr. Davis. You're back with us again, I see." She asked, "Do you think you can walk?" She gave him Ativan and a paper cup of water, and watched while he swallowed. Then she showed him to a room of his own.

HE KNEW

When he felt good, or even vaguely a little bit good, and sometimes even when he was not, by psychiatric standards, well at all, but nonetheless had a notion that he might soon be coming out of the Dread, as he called it, he insisted on taking Alice to Bergdorf Goodman, and afterward for a walk along Fifty-seventh Street, to Madison, where they would turn—this had become a tradition—and work their way north through the East Sixties and Seventies, into the low Eighties, touring the expensive shops. He was an occasional clotheshorse himself, of course, at times when he was not housebound in a bathrobe.

And it was one or the other, increasingly. The apartment or the square! He should have bought a place when he could have—he and Alice rented in the Village—back when he worked all the time instead of only rarely. But no, that wasn't the right attitude. Keep moving, he said to himself.

She was half a block ahead, across the street already, carrying her bags, which held the simple white blouse and the French lotions they'd bought for her. She was waiting for him to catch up. The light changed, and he crossed the street. He had a young wife. She didn't yet know what life had in store for her. Or did she?

He'd long ago been a competitive runner, and he sometimes thought about resuming his sport at the veteran level.
He'd been worrying about his heart, and it would do him
good. But he'd never do it. Or maybe he would.

She called out, "How do you get to stay so handsome?,"
and he was in love again. He trotted up the sidewalk and said,
"Ha, that's nice of you, but I'm overweight."

"Who cares? So am I," she proclaimed. "Look at my ass! I
need to get exercise."

"I love your ass," he said. "What do you see?" They were
standing in front of a boutique. She laughed. "We already have
enough Italian *sheets*!" There it was, the volume rising on the
last word, her shrill crescendo.

It was about the time of day when they should be choking
down a few pills. "We'll need to find some fluids before too
long," he said.

He put his arm around her shoulders and gently hugged
her. She arranged her shopping bags in one hand and wrapped
her other, free arm too tightly around his waist, steering him
up the block. They didn't fit well, walking so close—she
swung her butt, and their hips collided—and eventually they
drew apart and held hands. She had long dark hair and round
brown eyes, which, when he looked into them, seemed to
have other eyes behind them. What did he mean by that? It was
a feeling, hard to shape into words.

Thank God the money was holding out. He wasn't too
worried about their shopping. It had been his idea, to begin
with; it couldn't be laid at her feet, and, in fact, he wasn't
always spending on her. To do so, as was his intention that
afternoon, might implicate him in a father stereotype, it was
true, but who cared? It was a bright, cold Saturday, the last
Saturday in October—Halloween—and the light seemed
already to be fading toward night. Stephen had got himself
shaved and outdoors for the first time in two weeks, and

women wearing heels and men in European clothes were showing themselves in the uptown air.

"Can we stop here?" she said. They'd arrived at the lingerie store where, every year, before Christmas—usually at the last minute on Christmas Eve, at the end of one of his eleventh-hour gift-gathering runs—he came to buy her tap pants or a camisole, just as he'd done for his former wife on Christmases in years past. Marina, how was she? Was she still with Jeff?

"Let's go in and get you a pair of fishnets," he said, and they went in—the store was narrow—in single file. Two salesgirls were there to help them. One walked around the counter, toward Stephen, who raised his hands in the air, as if to prevent her from coming too close. Alice could easily be made upset if she thought she saw intimacy springing up between Stephen and another woman, even an attentive shop-girl or waitress, and he had learned to play down these innocent encounters. He announced to the women that he was shopping for his wife, and then put his arm around Alice and pulled her up beside him. "We'll need a tall size," he said.

He charged a pair of black woolen fishnets and two pairs of regular black stockings, and then they crossed the street and detoured off the avenue to look at a window display of men's suits. He had no need of one, and in fact hadn't bought one in quite some time, not since the world economy had taken its downturn.

"Let's keep moving," he said. A beautiful jacket in blue worsted wool was making him feel sad over—what? His reduced opportunities in life, probably. "How're you doing?" he asked Alice. "Are you holding up?" She was leaning against him. Here and there around them, babies, pushed in strollers, came and went.

"I'm holding up," she said.

The problem—the *problem*—was that he was no longer getting cast in the comic roles that had become, over years of acting in plays and, for a brief spell, on television, his strong suit. Or, no, maybe that wasn't the root problem. In a way, though, it was, in part because the dropoff in work and income had increased his normal daily load of terror, but also because his heartbreaking difficulties onstage had amplified his sense of himself, of his *Self*, he should say, as somehow consisting in, or activated by—what was a fitting way to put this?—the willing community made by the laughter of audiences.

"Will you please let me hold those for you?" he asked, and reached for Alice's shopping bags, the things he'd bought for her. She backed away from him quickly—had he startled her?—and said, "You're too slow, *man!*"

"You're right about that," he said.

"Come on! You're not even going to try?"

"Oh, God. You want me to fight you for the bags?"

"Yeah. Fight me."

"Are you fucking with me right now?" he said, in the snarl of a stock comic-melodrama villain. But this didn't come out funny—it was too unhinged-sounding, in tone and in volume—and her smile dropped, and she exclaimed, "Jesus, you don't need to freak *out!*"

She handed over the two purple bags and the one little black one, and they continued up Madison. They stopped for a light, and he asked her, "Are we skipping Barneys?" The entrance to the women's side of the department store was close by. Around the corner, over near Lexington Avenue, was the apartment of a hooker he'd visited in the nineties. Victoria.

What he hated about nice clothes was both wanting and not wanting to wear them. He disliked his own conspicuousness to himself, whenever he was out in the world expensively costumed. It was only the pleasure he felt in his tactile awareness of sewing and fabric, of the hands of the maker in the garment, that led him, again and again, to risk the danger of seeing himself—literally, reflected in the mirror of a bar, perhaps—as somehow faintly ridiculous.

It was an American problem, something that he felt only in America. He should have moved across the ocean when he'd had the chance, after his divorce from Marina. Though he'd never really had the chance. Where would he have gone? Rome? Berlin? London? How would he have worked? His old Neighborhood Playhouse friend Ned had decamped to the Netherlands some years back—when people still called it Holland—in order, Ned had told Stephen, to follow through on an artistic commitment to experimental performance, of which there always seemed to be so much in northern Europe; but then Stephen had heard through mutual acquaintances that Ned had married a Dutch woman, who'd helped him qualify for some form or other of enlightened state arts support, and that the two of them had taken to spending their days and nights smoking pot with expatriates in Amsterdam coffee shops, which sounded, to Stephen, both awful and wonderful.

"There's nothing at Barneys this season. Everything's got an Empire waist," Alice was telling him. She said, "That cut makes me feel like a little girl in an Easter dress. A giant little girl."

"It's not my favorite look," he agreed.

"It's all right on some people," she said, and he finished her thought for her, saying, "But not on you."

"Is it my tits? Are my tits too small? Is that the problem?"

"Take it easy. It's not your tits. Your tits are great," he said, and went on, "Those dresses are weird. You know what I mean? You're maybe a little too tall for an Empire waist, unless, I guess"—he made shapes with his hands in the air—"unless the skirt is very long."

It was how they'd met and fallen in love, five years before— her absurd height. Alice and Stephen had been invited to the same dinner party, for which they'd arrived at the same time. They got into the elevator together, and he pressed the button for their friends' floor, and she said, "That's me, too, thanks," and after that the doors closed and they avoided making eye contact, but on the way up they slipped and *saw* each other in the same instant and, in the shock of meeting her eyes, he exclaimed, in a whisper, "You're so tall!" and she blushed, and his face got red, too. Later that night, after they'd both drunk a lot of wine, while their hosts were clearing up, she confessed to him that, in the elevator, he'd uttered aloud her first, fleeting thought whenever she met anyone, which was that she was tall—her noticing of herself *being seen*, being taken in, was part of her appealing self-consciousness: It was her come-on, and it was working on him—and she'd added that (though Stephen had hardly been the first man to lead with a comment on her height) no one had ever read her mind in quite the way he seemed to have done.

That Halloween afternoon on Madison Avenue, she sounded mildly manic. "You're right! You're right, as always. It's not a big deal. I'm too tall for an Empire waist. It's as simple as that! I try and it doesn't work, and I try it and it doesn't work, and I should know better by now, because it's *obvious!*"

They were holding hands again. But he had a strong feeling that she was beginning to sink, that she was anxiously coming to feel and believe that she would somehow never be right. "Let's get you something to eat," he said, and she sighed and said, "Yeah, I'm starting to spin."

"I can hear it," he told her.

"You can?"

"Your Southern accent is coming out."

"I don't want to be too tall for you," she cried.

"You're not."

"I'm a wee bit dizzy."

"I'll hold you," he said.

A baby carriage was bearing down on them. He gripped her coat sleeve. On the next block, on the other side of Madison, was a coffee shop. He would have preferred a bar, but the one that he and Alice liked lay many blocks ahead. It wasn't yet time for drinking, anyway. He guided her off the curb, between two closely parked cars, and directly out into the open avenue—there was a moment, he figured, before the light changed and traffic surged forward—where he maneuvered her diagonally across against the wind that funneled down between the buildings. "We're almost there, come on," he called. He heard cars rushing up behind them. He sped her across the final lane, onto the sidewalk, and then ten feet more, to the door of the restaurant.

He held the door. "In you go," he said.

At the booth, he counted out pills, his antidepressants and her anti-anxieties—he carried and dispensed for her more often than not, ever since her suicide attempt—and he asked her, "How many do you think will do the trick? One? Two? Do you need two? Honey, can you talk?"

"Are those ten-milligram?"

"They are."

"Give me two. For now."

"Hang on."

"You're scattering them across the *table*!"

"Sorry. Sorry."

It was true, he'd dumped out a few too many pills, and some had rolled off toward the condiments, the ketchup and the sugar and the salt and pepper shakers and so forth, and he was missing—what was he missing? He had Alice's portion under control. And there were his pink-and-yellow antipsychotics. Where had his beta-blockers gone?

He peered up and saw that Alice's hair was a mess from

the wind. He could see the tension in her face—it always came on so swiftly and visibly. It was her terror of going back into the hospital. Her jaw had clenched, she was grinding her teeth, and the muscles in her neck were taut. "You're twisted up," he said, and reached across the table to help her adjust her clothes. Her cotton blouse had been pulled back over one shoulder when she'd taken off her coat, causing the shirt's brilliant mother-of-pearl buttons to look as if they were about to pop off at the collar.

He pushed two Valium tablets her way. Then he noticed Dr. Tillman, sitting alone at the counter, at the back of the restaurant.

The waitress arrived, and Alice said, "I'd like a Coca-Cola and a big piece of chocolate cake, but not the kind with raspberry filling."

Stephen said to Alice, "I think I see my former doctor over there," and Alice asked him rather too loudly if he was ready to order.

She told him, "You should eat something. If you don't, you're going to have a crash, and you're going to get all angry, and I don't want to be screamed at by you later on the street."

"Excuse me?"

He rolled his eyes at the waitress and blurted, "Ha, I don't know what to say to that!," but he felt embarrassed, and conceded to her, to the waitress, that he'd probably better have a muffin.

"Pumpkin, please," he added, and abruptly got up and pushed past her and escaped to the rear of the diner, calling, "Dr. Tillman? Dr. Tillman?" But the man didn't seem to hear him. Stephen came closer and got a better look at his old analyst, hunched over a plate of pancakes. Why was Dr. Tillman alone? Had his wife, whom Stephen had never met or even glimpsed, passed away? Dr. Tillman had to be in his eighties by now; he'd shrunk, of course, and his hair had finally gone fully white. And then Stephen remembered, shockingly, that Dr. Tillman had died six or seven or maybe eight years before. The man in the diner could never have been Dr. Tillman. Stephen marched off to the men's room, where he sat in a stall and checked his cell phone for text messages from his old friend Claire. Where was she? Had she gone to the country with Peter? He needed to talk to her—he needed her to calm him down—if only for a moment. It was a risky thing to do, with Alice so close by. Alice accepted as fact her suspicion that he and Claire had had an affair, several years back, during the months when Alice was hospitalized. They hadn't had an affair, actually, though for a while Claire had been important to him as a confidante. He'd fallen in love with her, a little, for her kindness, and, he told himself now, for her soft, deep voice, which always seemed to reassure him. He flushed, buckled, went back to the booth, and, thinking of Dr. Tillman, told Alice that he felt as if he'd seen a genuine ghost, and that he couldn't image how he'd forgotten the death of his psychiatrist of almost fifteen years, and that, although he understood that that time in his life, the time of his analysis with Dr. Tillman, was far in the past—or maybe because of this fact—he felt disoriented, weird.

"Welcome to the club," Alice replied. The Valium was doing its work. She already sounded slurry.

He said, "How's your chocolate cake?"

"Better than your muffin."

"You ate my muffin?"

"I didn't eat your muffin. It's sitting in front of you on your place mat."

"Right you are, there it is," he admitted.

He heard the sounds of a football game. Was there a television in the restaurant? It was the weekend of the Nebraska-Colorado game. Was it? Or, no, that game came closer to Thanksgiving.

"Are you all right?" she asked him.

He watched her eat. She'd scooped out all the cake and left a shell of frosting on her plate, which she'd saved for last. He watched her lick the icing off the tines of her fork. "Are you?" he asked her.

"I asked you first."

"I'm all right," he told her.

"Should I believe you?"

He picked up her medicine bottle, shook it gently, and dropped it into his sport coat's inside breast pocket.

"Are *you* all right?" he asked once more.

"I'm fine. I'm eating my lunch."

Later, back on the street, they made their way at a kind of wobbling pace uptown, toward the Whitney Museum. The sun was getting low in the sky. He said to her, "Alice, how many did you take?"

She was leaning hard on his shoulder, like a drunk date. They slowed to gaze at autumn scenery in the shop windows along the way. The first children wearing Halloween costumes had begun to appear on the avenue. Stephen saw a dragon, a skeleton, and several little princesses. He again asked Alice how many pills she'd sneaked while he was in the men's room.

"Five?" Her voice sounded like a young girl's.

"Five in all? Or five plus the two I gave you?"

"Five in all. Three more."

He shifted her shopping bags from his left hand to his right, and offered her his other shoulder. Supporting her weight, block after block, wasn't easy, and at Seventy-third Street he insisted that they get in a cab, go straight home, and tuck her into bed for the rest of the day.

But she simply apologized for letting her anxiety get the better of her. She said that she was also sorry for provoking him, in the restaurant, with her fear that he might yell at her if he didn't eat properly. She hadn't meant to shame him. She loved him. She wanted them to have a fantastic time out in the world. That was all that mattered.

More children, herded by parents and nannies, ran past them, trick-or-treating, hitting the boutiques. The costumes were good. A few—in particular, a spectacular lion suit on a four- or five-year-old boy—looked to have been sewn with care, showing a level of detailing appropriate to durable stage costumes, the sort meant for nightly scrutiny under theater lights.

When Stephen was younger, when he was a young actor, working in his costume for the first time—putting it on before the call for the first dress rehearsal—had always been a revelation. This was the case for many actors, certainly. Wearing the garment was an acquisition of—why not say it?—humanity. A Victorian frock coat or a pair of Windsor-style stovepipe trousers or even Depression-era dungarees, worn *as* a character, could in turn produce character. When Stephen put on a costume, he could feel his whole nervous system, his muscles, and his bones, rearranging themselves to form his character's body and posture. For instance, the heavy woolen overcoat worn by a foolish servant caused a slump in the shoulders and an itchy stiffness in the neck that might seem to an audience to be the symptoms of a master's beatings. The drama became palpable through tailoring. Maybe it followed that Stephen's life seemed to gain grace and substance when he walked at an even pace on a nice street in well-cut pants.

She wasn't letting him do this. Both of her arms were wrapped around him. Alice was hugging him tightly from the side, and they'd become like two people in a three-legged race at a county fair or family reunion. Neither of them had much in the way of family. She'd come to the city from North Carolina, as had he. They'd grown up in neighboring valleys in the Smoky Mountains, though he'd left home—he was gone before his eighteenth birthday—before she was even born. Their somewhat shared origins had, of course, been a crucial factor in their romance. (It wasn't her body alone that had attracted him, that night at the dinner party; nor had she truly believed, when he spoke to her in the elevator, that he was an actual mind reader.) For the first year or two of their relationship, they'd discussed plans to rent a convertible and drive south together through New Jersey and Delaware and Maryland, continuing around Washington and on through the Shenandoah Valley, in Virginia—there was a nineteenth-century inn near Staunton that he'd read about in a food mag-azine and wanted to spend a night or two at—and then from there into the southerly regions of the Blue Ridge, where, taking their time, they'd leave the interstate and get on the old two-lane, hairpin-turn state and county road that would take them up and across the mountains, to home. But they hadn't done it.

They hadn't done it because there was no one there for them. His parents were dead, and he had no aunts or uncles left, either. He had only a sister, who lived in Minnesota. Ste-phen and his sister had less and less to do with each other these days, and it had been at least a couple of decades since he had heard from, or thought to be in touch with, any of their remaining kin, the more or less distant cousins, who (some of them, at least) were surely still scattered about the countryside around Asheville. Alice's situation wasn't much happier. Her father, an alcoholic, had left her mother when Alice was four, and the man whom Alice had grown up calling father had been killed in an automobile accident when she was sixteen. Her mother, in later years, had become one of those people who try new places again and again, endlessly relocating. Currently she was parked outside Fort Worth. Alice had an unmarried, born-again brother who repaired computers in Sacramento.

Stephen turned to face her. Adjusting himself wasn't easy to do; they were pressed together, and his arms were pinned at his sides by her close embrace. Her clothes remained as they'd been in the restaurant, tugged slightly askew, and strands of her hair, caught between their bodies, were pulled when he moved. "Ouch!" she said.

She looked good—no, great. That she was so attractive while sedated troubled him. Did he like her best when she was out of it? "I know exactly the thing to do," he said, and she whispered, "What's that?"

"Let's go buy you a hat."

"A hat!" she said.

"Would you like that?"

"Yes."

"You'll have to let me move. Let go, all right?" he asked. But she didn't release him. The boy in the fancy lion suit bolted from a store's open doorway, and Alice said, "Oh, honey."

She wasn't talking to Stephen. She was peering down at the boy, who'd stopped short on the sidewalk in order to roar at them.

"Are you a *lion*?" Alice asked. "What kind of lion are you? Are you a fierce"—she paused; it was the Valium—"lion?"

"Yes," the lion growled, though not very fiercely.

Here came the father, calling, "Baby girl, baby girl, where are you going? Don't run off! Come take Daddy's hand. Leave those people alone."

The man was about thirty-five or maybe thirty-eight or nine years old, forty or so, and his wife was coming up behind.

"Sorry about that, please excuse us," the lion's father said.

The man's wife looked plain, with short brown hair and a small chin, though, on the other hand, she was attractive. "Don't be a bother," she instructed her daughter. She was English. Both she and her husband were conservatively dressed. The man was frankly, openly appraising Alice. Did this entitled young punk think that greater age made Stephen weak? He said to the parents, "I was noticing what a finely made costume your little girl is wearing. She looks so ferocious in it, I was certain she was a boy."

"Girls can't be ferocious, then?" the mother said, and her mildly accusing tone made Stephen unsure how to take this. Was it a reprimand, and, if so, was it also a flirtation?

A low mood was creeping on him. "Of course girls can be ferocious," Stephen replied. "My name is Stephen." He held out his hand and said, "And this is my ferocious wife, Alice." Alice was still leaning on his shoulder, with her right arm wrapped around his neck. Her body, against his, seemed to be sliding toward the pavement.

"I'm Margaret," the English wife said, and her American husband followed: "Robert. It's nice to meet you."

The mother said, "Claire, can you say hello to these nice people?" Stephen felt a sharp tremor in Alice, and he thought, Fuck, why *that* name?

Together, as if on cue, they all peered down at the daughter. The girl was slowly turning, spinning in a circle inside the cage of legs that had formed around her when the adults squared off to shake hands.

"Don't spill your candy, dear," her mother said.

The lion girl looked at her mom. She checked in with Dad. She seemed quite drawn to Alice, whose gaze she held a long moment.

"Claire, please say hello," her mother said again.

"Claire!" her father ordered.

Stephen could feel Alice clinging to him and pulling away at the same time.

"Hello," the little girl said, and Stephen loudly blurted, "And how old are *you*?"

"Five."

"Five!" he exclaimed.

"We're in kindergarten, aren't we?" her mother said to her, and went on, "It takes her a while to feel comfy with strangers."

"I understand," Stephen said, and wondered what Margaret and Robert were thinking of him and Alice. What picture did they make, this older man worrisomely buoying up his sedated young wife? His anxiety was on the rise, the sun was setting in earnest, the temperature was falling, and the wind was building. He might need to sneak one or two of Alice's Valiums. He spoke for them as a couple. "It's awfully nice to have met you and your lovely daughter, but we should get going."

And to Alice he proposed, brightly, "Hey, we're looking for a hat for you, remember?"

But before they could make their getaway Margaret announced to her husband, "Oh, Rob! I know who he is!"

"You were on that TV show," she said to Stephen. "Am I right? What was the show called? Was that you?"

"It may have been me, yes."

"You were that friend of the main character who was always causing mischief for everyone."

"Get out of my way," Stephen said.

"What?" the husband said.

"The show was called *Get Out of My Way*," Stephen explained, and added, "That was a long time ago. I'm amazed that you recognized me."

"You were very funny."

"Thank you."

To her husband, Margaret said, "Do you remember that show, dear?" And he answered, "No, I don't."

"He's not much for television," she said to Stephen, in a low, confiding tone. "Are you on something now?" she asked, and he thought to make a joke about his meds.

"No. I've been on a hiatus."

"Refueling your creativity?"

"Something like that."

"And are you an actress?" Margaret was addressing Alice. Stephen said, "Alice, she's asking you."

Sleepy Alice replied, "Oh, no."

"My wife is also between things," he said, and then, stupidly, he remarked to Alice, "We're taking some time to enjoy our lives, right?" He gave her a squeeze, and she glared at him.

Later, after they'd finally got free and resumed their trek up Madison Avenue, she accused him: "You were flirting with her."

"What? I wasn't."

"She's the type for you. Refueling your creativity."

"Come on, let's get you home."

"I don't have a *home*!"

"Yes, you do, you have a home with me."

They'd been lost in these woods before.

"How many pills did you take, Alice? Will you tell me how many pills you took? You took more than five, Alice. Please don't lie to me. How many?"

She wasn't talking. They passed shop after shop, but she didn't want him to go into any of them. She'd pulled away at last and was walking faster, out ahead of him now, fleeing. He buttoned up his coat and pulled off his scarf—it was the blue scarf that she'd given him in the first year of their marriage; he loved it and wore it all the time in the colder months—and ran up beside her and wrapped it around her neck. He said, emphatically, "Alice, nothing ever happened between me and Claire. Nothing was ever going to happen," which was true, though Alice would not believe it. Alice had met Claire and found her to be very beautiful. She suspected that Stephen would be more comfortable, more at home, with a woman closer to him in age—Stephen and Claire had gone to college together. Alice had conceived of Stephen's betrayal in the days before her breakdown, and, once in the hospital, when she'd been unable to simply go to a phone in the night and call him, the idea of their affair had grown in her; to this day, he could not say with certainty whether she'd tried to kill herself over her anticipated abandonment or whether that deranging fantasy had been a symptom of some deeper despair. It haunted them still.

Alice said, "Don't blow up at me."

"I'm not."

"You're shouting."

"Alice, I love you! Please try to take that in!" he shouted, and then quickly glanced around to see if he'd been heard by people passing by. In a lowered voice he said, "Why must we always return to this?"

"You were sleeping with her when I was on a locked ward! I thought my life was over! Where were *you*?" she pleaded.

"I was with you every day, Alice. I visited you every single day."

"And then you went to her!" she said angrily. Now he could hear and feel her terror, and he, too, began to feel frightened, because he knew where this fight could take them.

"Alice, stop this," he commanded.

"Leave me, just leave me already," she cried, and he watched as she ran away, up the block and across Seventy-ninth Street.

"Alice!" he called. But she was still going, a dark shape charging unsteadily up the street with her shopping bags.

It was the time of day when the lights from apartment buildings and stores began to shine brightly. Through the pools of light spilling out of shop doors came people in costume, not only children but adults, on their way to Halloween parties and bars. He forged ahead against a tide of ghosts and pirates and sexy nurses from the spirit realm. He passed a shattered Marilyn Monroe, but could no longer see Alice in the distance. With hands trembling, he took her pills from his coat pocket, opened the lid, and shook out two. Did he need one or two? It was the same question he'd asked Alice earlier in the coffee shop.

He put one in his mouth and another in his shirt pocket, in case. His mouth was parched from his own medications. He held the pill under his tongue. Eventually it would dissolve. He had only to wait.

He would wait at their bar. Maybe she was there already, he thought, as he turned the corner and left the avenue.

The place was a carnival inside. Cardboard witches and crepe-paper bats hung from the ceiling, and candlelit jack-o'-lanterns had been set out on the marble surface of the bar. Everyone inside was costumed, to some degree, but in his agitation Stephen imagined that it was actually he, in his soft windowpane jacket and pressed shirt and woolen pants—he and not the dead and undead thronging about him, blocking his way—who was wearing a costume. Through the crowd he pushed, searching for her. Finally he gave up and went to the bar, where he leaned into a gathering of wraiths and ordered a bourbon from a pretty bartender with a blood-red slash impastoed darkly across her neck.

The Valium was starting to help. He drank, and the alcohol burned his throat. When a seat became free, he took it immediately and ordered another bourbon, before locating his phone and dialing Alice's number.

"You can run a tab," he told the bartender, and added, "I could use some water, too, when you get a minute."

Outside in the night, he thought, Alice would be walking, disoriented. She'd be feeling scorned. She would hear her phone ringing in her purse and know it was him, but she'd be unable to answer, though she badly wanted to. She'd be afraid of him pulling her back, afraid of going childless all her life and winding up a widow, like her mother, running from place to place and never stopping. He'd heard all of this played out before.

Of course, he'd told her again and again that he wanted to have a baby with her. Why hadn't it happened already? Why hadn't they yet done it, like normal people?

He pictured her gathering her coat around her and slumping on a town-house stoop, ignoring his calls, or, likely, though by now she knew better than to expect a helpful response, calling her mother.

When he dialed her number for the fifth or sixth time, Alice answered. He told her that he was in their bar and felt desperate. "Come back," he said. "Will you?"

"Are you having a drink?" she asked.

"I am," he said. He pressed his phone hard against his ear. Loudly, above the bar chaos, he asked her, "Where are you? Do you know where you are? Do you need me to come get you?"

"No," she said. She hadn't gone far; she was only around the corner from where they always wound up at the end of these days when he took her out and bought her gifts.

She said that she was on her way, and a few minutes later he saw her appear behind him in the antique saloon mirror above the bar. She peered over the crowd of monsters and ghouls, his statuesque, distraught Alice, until she caught sight of him, his reflection and hers making contact in the glass.

He stood and said, "Excuse me, excuse me," to some skeletons and ghosts who were clustered between them. He opened a path for her and led her back to his seat. The goblin who'd been sitting beside him at the bar, when he saw Alice in her very real anguish, said, politely, "Oh, here, please, sit," and Stephen said, "Thank you," and nestled in beside his wife and let her rest her head on his shoulder. Gently, she cried. He wrapped one arm around her shoulders, and with his other hand he stroked her hair, pressing her close to him, so that her cheek lay against his heart. The bartender approached, but he gestured at her to give them time, another minute, then picked up his drink and brought it to Alice's lips, saying, "Here, love, it's okay, it's okay."

"I'm scared," she said.

He let her drink, then put the glass on the bar and, with his fingers, softly massaged away the mascara that had run in streams down her cheeks. For a while, they stayed together like that. He ordered a drink for her, and another for himself, and, little by little, she regained herself and was able to sit up straight. "I'm sorry," she said to him, and he said, "I'm sorry, too," and she asked, "Can you forgive me for running away?" and he said, "Alice. I don't want anyone but you."

"Do you mean it?" she said.

"More than anything," he answered. He said, "I know what we need to do. We need to take a vacation. We need to take our trip to the mountains. Let's do it. If we go soon, we'll still be in time to see the autumn leaves."

They talked about the trip, what kind of car they'd rent—not a convertible at this time of year, certainly—and about how many days they might spend in this place or that; and they wondered together what they'd find, after so many years away, of their old home towns and the houses in which they'd grown up. He held her hand tightly in his as they spoke, and she remembered something she'd never told him before. There had been a spring that made a little swimming hole in the woods behind her house. It had been a secret place for her—she hadn't even told her brother about it. Would it still be there? Would it have been bulldozed for a strip mall or a retirement community or a new drive-through bank? Would she be able to find it again?

"Let's go there," he said, and with that he left three twenty-dollar bills on the bar and stood up and put on his coat and helped her to stand. He buttoned her coat for her and wrapped his scarf in a knot around her collar. He picked up her bags and took her by the hand and led her carefully through the Halloween necropolis. They were the only two regular-looking people in the place.

Outside, he hailed a cab. He held the door for her, then got in beside her and gave the address, and they rode down Fifth Avenue, past Central Park and the Plaza and Tiffany & Co., and Cartier and Rockefeller Center and Saks, down through the Forties and the Thirties and the Twenties, to Washington Square Park, the very bottom of the avenue, and west from there into the Village. She leaned on him as they climbed the four flights to their walk-up. He unlocked and pushed open the door. He turned on a light and guided her through the living room and into their bedroom, where he turned on the little lamp beside the bed. He took her coat and sat her on the edge of the bed and knelt on the floor in front of her. He started tugging off her clothes—first her shoes, then her skirt and her stockings. "Raise your arms, baby," he said, and pulled her blouse up and over her head. He un-snapped her bra and took that, too. He helped her to lie down. He pulled the covers over her, and then undressed himself, switched off the lamp, and went unclothed into the living room, where he sat on the sofa, absently touching and spin-ning the gold ring on his finger. After a while, he got up and turned off the living-room light and made his way quietly back to her in the dark. He raised the covers and got into bed beside her and brought her close, spooning, so that he could cup her breasts in his hands and feel the length of her body against his.

In the morning, he told himself before falling asleep, they would sit naked beside each other, resting against pillows, drinking coffee in bed—his black, hers with milk—and he would speak to her openly and forthrightly about getting his acting career back on track; and before long they would kiss, and when they made love he would drive hard into her and come, hoping, hoping for her pregnancy, for the child, their son, perhaps—a boy like him!—and believing as best he could that their family was drawing close, was near at last.

EVER SINCE

Ever since his wife had left him—but she wasn't his wife, was she? he'd only thought of her that way, had begun to think of her that way, since her abrupt departure, the year before, with Richard Bishop—Jonathan had taken up a new side of his personality and become the sort of lurking man who, say, at work or at a party, mainly hovers on the outskirts of other people's conversations, leaning close but not *too* close, listening in while gazing out vaguely over their heads in order to seem distracted and inattentive, waiting for the conversation to wind down, so that he can weigh in gloomily and summarize whatever has just been said.

He was at it again.

"What you're saying, if I've heard you right, is that the current rates of city government spending will eventually bankrupt the public schools." He was speaking to a group of young parents—presumably, that's what they were—at a book-publication party for a novelist he'd never read. He'd come with his friend, his date, he should say, who worked for the novelist's publisher. He added, "My ex-wife, well, not my wife, but, you know, she might as well have been, taught eighth grade in the Bronx for two years."

"Really?" a woman in the group asked. The man next to

Jonathan turned sideways, as if he were a door swinging open to let him in.

Jonathan stepped forward. "Yes. She found it exhausting but exhilarating. She loved her students but always felt at war with the administration. Finally, she quit. It made her depressed."

"I can see how it might be depressing to teach in the New York public schools," the man who'd moved to let Jonathan into the circle said. "But it's important work."

Jonathan said, "That's how Rachel felt, and that was the pity of it. Every day was a struggle for her, because she believed in what she was doing." In this way he invoked her, as he often did, in heroic terms. Thinking of her in a grandiose light made him want to cry for what he'd lost in her, and he lowered his head and quietly announced, "Excuse me, it's been nice talking to you all." Without waiting for introductions, he headed off to the bar, where he asked the bartender for "Scotch and soda on the rocks? Please?"

Where was Sarah? He couldn't see her in the crowd. This party was a work night for her. It was important that he not get too drunk.

But it had been one of those weeks, and he wanted a cigarette. There had to be smokers somewhere, clustered together in a stairwell or guest bedroom, or craning out of one of the giant loft's windows overlooking the Hudson. The sun setting behind industrial New Jersey was brightly orange and enormous. He heard Sarah's voice, and turned. "I've been looking all over for you. I'm running away from my boss."

"I'll bet you are," he said.

"She wants me to be paying attention to this obnoxious writer we're celebrating tonight."

"Tell me again the name of his book?"

"*The Strictures of My Love.*"

"Right."

"He's very demanding. He wants a lot of publicity. He's a twerp. But he makes money for the company."

Publicity was Sarah's area.

"Give me a sip of your drink," she said, and Jonathan handed her his glass.

"I was looking for a place to smoke," he said.

"Did you bring cigarettes?"

"No, I was going to bum one."

"Bum two, will you?" she said, and gave him back his Scotch and soda. The ice in the glass was already melting. "I'll come find you. I have to make an effort to be professional." He watched her sashay off toward the author, who was surrounded by guests and was wearing a suit. Really, he should marry Sarah, he reminded himself. But, then again, he should've married Rachel.

Now waiters were making their rounds with trays. Jonathan took something off one of the trays and wound up holding a toothpick, which he put in his shirt pocket, next to the joint he'd rolled that afternoon in a stall in the men's room at his office. Was it time for another drink? The last shindig Sarah had brought him to—it had been on the Upper West Side, near Columbia University, for a historian of the Revolution— he'd remained sober and later wondered why.

On his way back to the bar, he saw Fletcher, a young editor at Sarah's company, who, according to Sarah, bombarded her with daytime e-mails asking for dates that she then declined. Fletcher was thinner than he—in better shape all around, no doubt—with sharp cheekbones and a widow's peak.

"Jonathan," Fletcher was saying.

"Hi, Fletcher."

"It looks like we're both en route to the bar."

"Or the bathroom."

"Good point," Fletcher said, and Jonathan said, "I think you're right, though. The bar." Then a pretty girl walked past, and the energy in the room seemed to rise. The men got their drinks refreshed and went off in different directions.

The loft was filling and growing noisier. Next to Jonathan, people were talking animatedly about health-care reform—a woman in the group who'd undergone surgery was deep in debt. Jonathan craned his neck and blurted, "The possibilities for real change in health care are undercut by the bureaucracies that make change crucial! My ex-wife used to talk about this all the time." Then, shyly, he added, as he always did, "Actually, she wasn't my wife, but we were together for many years."

"It's nice to meet you," a man wearing a pale-green shirt said. "I'm William, and this is Kathy, and this is Deborah." It was Kathy, a short blonde, who had had the surgery.

Jonathan nodded and said, "My name is Jonathan. I hope it wasn't rude of me to jump in like that."

"What's a party for?" Kathy said, and then asked, "Do you know a lot about the medical industry?"

"Not really," Jonathan admitted. "Rachel—that's the woman I wasn't married to—had strong opinions on social issues."

"I'm ready for another drink!" William announced.

"Get me a white wine?" Deborah asked.

"I'll go with you," Jonathan, who had been sipping constantly, said. He looked around for Rachel—no, Sarah—but didn't see her.

At the bar he told William, "I'm not of this world."

"Excuse me?"

"I mean, I'm here with a friend."

"Aren't we all?" William said. "Cheers." He carried his drink and Deborah's wine back into the crowd.

The summer sun had nearly set. The light it threw into the loft had become an amber glow that shone up through the windows to touch the ceiling, where it outlined the shadows of party guests. Soon, as night fell, the loft's numerous wall sconces would come on. Copies of the author's books were stacked in little piles everywhere.

Jonathan was extremely conscious of his origins, which were Southern, his father and his father's family having come from Virginia, and his mother and hers from the Florida Gulf Coast. Jonathan's father had been dead for ten years, and his mother had retired to Maryland's Eastern Shore; and, these days, he regarded himself as oddly and bravely homeless, imagining, from this city he'd chosen to live in, a lost, green place—Charlottesville, where his parents had been professors, and the nearby Blue Ridge, where he'd camped as a boy. If he drank enough, his accent would break through.

Sarah appeared at his side. "Hey, buster, let's go fuck in the bathroom," she said. That was something that he loved about her—her easy playfulness, which he took as a sign not only of her trust in him but also of her willingness to let him trust her. "I wish we could," he told her, though in fact he didn't, at that moment, wish so—he needed a smoke more.

"Are you done taking care of the writer?" he asked.

"I was finished with that a long time ago," she said.

She was shorter than Jonathan by a foot. When they walked down the street together, and he rested his arm on her shoulder, he thought sometimes about how essential it would be in old age to have someone to lean on. And though his old age was a long way off, and he felt, the majority of the time, that he would never reach it anyway, he nonetheless considered it often when he was with Sarah.

"How are you and Fletcher getting on?" he asked.

"We're fine," she said.

"I saw him earlier. He's not very talkative."

"Come with me—there's something I want to show you." She took Jonathan's hand and tugged him toward the windows.

He said, "Hang on, I want to get a drink."

"You've got a drink."

"It's about gone."

"Get it in a minute," she pleaded. "We'll get drinks to-gether and then find somewhere to hide out."

She was in love with him. It pulled at him, as if with a kind of warm, perfumed gravity.

What she had to show him was the sun, disappearing at last, and the sky above, the color of fire. She held his hand, as they stood together before a big window, and he wished that he were more in love with her. Or was he, maybe, in love with her?

She said, "The world is incredible at this time of day, isn't it?"

"It is," he agreed, and took a step back from the windows. He said, "A lot of the color in the air is the product of atmospheric pollutants." He felt her hand go limp in his. He apologized. "I didn't mean anything by that."

She was easily upset. He often found himself apologizing to her for remarks that he hadn't meant to be hurtful. She squeezed his hand, and he squeezed hers, and he felt, for just an instant, at peace.

Things at the party were picking up. Jonathan faintly smelled cigarette smoke. "Come on, sweet pea," he said to Sarah, and pulled her away from the window and back to the bar.

They took their drinks and went to stand in a corner, and Sarah said, "So, mister, what about us?"

Was she a little drunk?

"Us," he said. But before he could go on there was a loud crash in the middle of the room, followed by a hasty shuffling of partygoers turning around, making space for the accident, the mishap—someone had tripped over a piece of furniture and fallen heavily. It was William, the man in the green shirt. "I'm all right, I'm all right," Jonathan heard him saying as he

rose to his knees, then his feet. "I'm only suffering minor em-
barrassment," he said, laughing, as, behind him, a man in
gray—it was the celebrated author—pushed the chair William
had tripped on back into its place beside the long glass-topped
coffee table.

"Is he good?" Jonathan asked Sarah.

"Who?"

"The author. Is he good?"

"People think so."

"Rachel read one of his books."

"Which one?"

"I don't remember," Jonathan said, but amended, "Oh, no,
I almost remember. It had 'kill' in the title."

"*Abel Kills Cain*," Sarah said.

"It sounds like the name of a band."

"It should be."

"Hey, I like this guy," Jonathan said.

She joked, "Don't say that until you've worked with him,"
and Jonathan said, "No, not the writer. I mean the guy who fell.
He's coming over here."

Then William was upon them.

"How bad did that look?" he asked.

Jonathan said, "William, this is Sarah. Sarah, William."
Then he said, "It didn't look bad."

"From your lips to God's ears."

"As long as you're not hurt, that's all that matters," said
Sarah.

"Hurt my body all you want, but leave my pride alone,"
William said, and Sarah replied, "I *know* what you mean."

She was a touch drunk.

It was the three of them now, snaking in a line past artworks and tall bookshelves, searching for smokers. They stopped
at a door that was locked, and kept going, single file, with
Jonathan leading and Sarah in the middle. At times the crowd

pressed in, and Jonathan had to forge a path through it. They came to an open door that led into a hallway painted dark red, and could hear voices down the hall.

"Who lives here?" William asked.

"The owner is the heir to a cosmetics fortune," Sarah said, adding, "He's also a very good poet."

At the end of the hall was a room, where about eight people were gathered on and around a big bed, talking and drinking.

"Come in!" a comfortably stretched-out man, who had taken off his shoes, cried. "We're having an argument about whether it's ethical to live on government disability in your twenties."

Right away, Jonathan said, "It is if you're disabled. My ex-wife used to work with disabled kids." Then, for Sarah's sake, he anxiously exclaimed, "I don't mean my ex-wife! I don't know why I said that!"

"We're not talking about *that* kind of disabled," the man said.

"My friends and I were looking for a place to smoke," Jonathan quickly replied.

"I think people were smoking on the terrace," the man said.

"There's a terrace?" Jonathan asked.

"I know where it is," William said.

It was William's turn to lead. They went back out and along the red hallway to the main room, and then squeezed and pushed their way diagonally through the crowd toward the terrace door. Now when Jonathan tried to touch Sarah's shoulder, or hold her hand, she pulled away. As they were about to reach the terrace, she spun around, shouting above the party noise, "Your ex-*wife*?"

"I'm sorry. That was a slip."

"She was your *wife*? Are you out of your mind? She was

never your wife!" Then Sarah asked him, "Do you still love her?" But she didn't wait for him to answer. She said, "I don't even want to know."

"I'm sorry. I'm very sorry."

"I'll think about it," Sarah said.

William held the door, and she marched out onto the hot, humid terrace. Jonathan skulked behind her.

He and she and William sprawled on the patio furniture and waited for smokers, but none came. The terrace faced north, toward midtown. A large ascending moon, glowing in the sky over the Rockaways, was partly visible around the corner of the building.

"Ought I to light a joint?" Jonathan asked—now a trace of his Southern diction emerged—and William said, "Absolutely," but Sarah, still angry, said, "Save it for later."

He could feel a light breeze. He felt the joint in his shirt pocket. He'd known her in a distant way, through other people, mutual friends, for a long, long time—when had they first met? It had been at the wedding of his college classmate Kenneth—and they'd run into each other here and there in the ten or eleven years since, either at parties or in big groups at restaurants, that sort of thing; and, at any rate, this drawn-out, vague acquaintance had given them each the subtle feeling, once they'd begun seeing each other and sleeping together, that they somehow shared common origins, though in fact she'd grown up on the Upper East Side, the daughter of psychoanalysts, and showed a dedication to European fashion magazines—Rachel had rejected fashion as a malignant form of commercialism—that he would never, throughout their long life ahead, their marriage, come to fathom.

He overheard her whispering to William but couldn't make out what she was saying. She and William were on a pair of low lounge chairs, off a ways from his. Above the brick terrace wall, he could see the spire of the Empire State Building.

Below that, on the terrace, was Sarah's back, turned to him. He had a view of her ass, wrapped in her cotton skirt. How much had she drunk?

Finally the terrace door opened and more people tumbled out, including William's friends.

"We came to find you!" Kathy exclaimed, and Deborah said, "Here you are! Where have you been?"

"Exploring!" William said, then went on, "Deborah, Kathy, this is Sarah, my new pal, and you met Jonathan earlier."

"Hi, hi," everyone said.

Jonathan had the feeling—he was drunk enough to feel this—that, though they were all just casually meeting, they were also, after a stretch of being apart, coming into one another's company *again* in a significant way: The encounter on the terrace was a homecoming.

"Is anyone smoking?" he asked, and Deborah felt about in her purse and said, "Where are my cigarettes? I just had them."

The terrace was filling. Everywhere, people were gathering in groups of two and three and four.

Deborah practically screamed at him, "I'm sorry, I don't know where my pack went!" and Jonathan said, "We'll find some."

He called, "Sarah, come sit with me," but Sarah turned her head and said, "In a minute. I'm talking to William."

With Rachel, all his pent-up urges to make a home and a family had begun to declare themselves—in his last year with her he'd felt a strong desire to have a child. At times this desire had come on him fiercely. He'd felt it as a pleasurable shock that rose from his knees up through his chest to the top of his head, causing him to tremble and sometimes visibly shudder. He recalled that Rachel, early in their relationship, had had an intuition that, were they to have a child, it would be a daughter. This idea of a girl had settled in him, and after a while he couldn't conceive of a son. When Rachel left him for Richard Bishop, he'd felt bereft not only of her, of his never-to-be wife, but of the daughter that they had not had, would not have; and now a year had passed, during which he'd often felt that his chances at fatherhood had gone with her, with Rachel. Of course, this wasn't true, he knew that, but the feeling was convincing, and much of the time he went about in a state of grief over it.

He had to take action. He would go hunting and bring back a cigarette for Sarah. He got up from the chaise and said, "Deborah, come on, let's go find cigarettes." He held the door for her, and she went inside ahead of him.

"Where are we going?" she asked.

She had dyed red hair and pale skin. She was about Rachel's height and size. He hadn't looked closely at her earlier, when William had first introduced them.

"I'm not sure," he said. What was he doing with this woman? "We're going to the bar," he said.

"Lead the way," Deborah said, and he squeezed by her and got in front, where he set to work. At one point, he got them stuck—the crowd was thick indeed—and he heard a man near him say, "You can't just drop a bunch of rocks in a pile to make a stone wall. There's a way to do it. It isn't random."

They backtracked. Now Jonathan was following. Deborah found a path and got them to the bar. She was drinking vodka.

"What do you do?" he asked.

"I'm an architect."

"Really? What kinds of things do you build?"

"I mostly work on apartment renovations. I've done some house additions. How about you?"

"I'm a lawyer," he said.

"What kind?"

"I do litigation."

"I like your jacket," she said, and reached out and felt the sleeve.

"Oh, thanks, thank you," he said.

Behind her, he saw Fletcher, gazing over at them. Jonathan turned his body away from Deborah's. He spoke to the bartender. "Is there a back stairwell somewhere, or a fire exit?"

"Try the kitchen," the bartender said.

Jonathan could see the tops of two swinging doors opening and closing about twenty feet away. He could see Fletcher approaching.

He grabbed Deborah's hand and pulled her forcibly toward the kitchen doors. "I think it's over in this direction," he said.

Deborah exclaimed, "I'm right here!"

"Sorry, I was trying to avoid someone," he said.

They waited for a man carrying a tray to pass, and then went into the kitchen.

"Can I help you, sir?" a waiter asked.

"We're looking for the stairs."

The waiter pointed past a long kitchen island lined with trays and overhung with copper and steel pots.

"Make room, make room, please," a waitress called as she walked by. There was a smell of baking bread.

Jonathan said, "Let's go," and he and Deborah rounded the kitchen island. He opened the heavy steel door at the back, near the freezer.

"Aw, fuck," he said.

The gray stairwell was empty. The door closed behind them and they stood face-to-face under the dim light. Peering at Deborah in the dark put him in mind of Rachel; suddenly he wanted to call her, a bad idea.

Deborah was holding his sleeve again. "Hey," she said. "How are you doing?"

"All right."

"I like you," she said then.

"I like you, too," he said, and she announced, "I want you to know that if we sleep together and get pregnant I'm keeping the baby."

He frantically wrenched the door open.

"I don't know what to say! It used to be that people always smoked in the fire exit!" he blurted.

Where was Sarah? He needed to put things right with her. He stormed out of the kitchen and through to the terrace. On his way, he noticed that a few people at the center of the room had begun subtly dancing to the music playing on the stereo. Sarah was no longer on the terrace. The moon was higher in the sky now. Instead of a dying sunset, he saw in the west a bright metropolis of oil tanks, freeways, and planes taking off or landing at Newark. He'd lost Deborah—abandoned her, really—along the way. Back into the party he went. Then, at a loss over how the evening was going, he made for the front door and the antique cage elevator, which he rode to the lobby with a couple who were leaving the party—but what was *he* doing? Was he also leaving?

He was. The heat on the street had made a soup of the air. He felt his hair sticking to his forehead. He looked at his phone. He was on the verge of being quite drunk. He put the phone back in his pocket. This was his way of not calling Rachel.

He began walking. There was nothing much to look at on the street: bagged trash and a few brightly lit entryways. He came to a broad artery. Church Street? He was sweating. A couple passed him.

He and Sarah made a couple, didn't they? Was it too late to phone Rachel? He crossed Church. After another few blocks, he had a feeling that the street was sloping downward.

There was the river. He leaned heavily against a building and dialed, and Rachel answered. "Jonathan?"

"Hey. Is it all right that I called?"

"Not really."

"Can you talk?"

"Maybe for a minute."

"I've been missing you."

Rachel said, "You shouldn't be calling me, Jonathan."

"I know." The buildings around him were massive and dark.

"Have you been drinking?" she asked.

"Some."

"Oh, Jonathan."

"What?"

"Jonathan, we've been over everything. We don't have anything to talk about anymore."

"You're right."

"I was ready to marry you," she said.

"Why are you bringing that up?"

"Because you were never going to ask."

"You don't know that," he said. Then he said, angrily, "Hang on, a truck is going by; I can't hear you."

"Can you hear me now?"

"Yes," he said, and she asked, "Where are you?"

He said, "Downtown, near the Hudson," and she said, "Jonathan, I think I should tell you that Richard and I are moving."

"Moving? You're moving? Where?"

"Los Angeles. He has some friends who can hook him up with teaching work at one of the art colleges."

"Oh."

"I thought you might have heard from Irena or Paul."

"What?"

"I said, I thought you might have heard from Irena or Paul."

"I haven't talked to either of them."

"Let's not fight," she said.

"I'm not fighting!" he said with a raised voice, and she said, "I heard that you've been seeing someone."

"Oh, God, Rachel," he whimpered. He was suddenly near tears.

"I'm sorry," she said.

Then he began to weep. He tried to keep the sound from her. She said, again, "I'm sorry. I'm so sorry, Jonathan."

Jonathan put his phone back in his pocket. He wiped his wet eyes with his jacket sleeve and thought of Sarah.

By the time he got back up the street to the building, he had pulled himself together. The loft was a mess. The author's books had disappeared or been scattered. The music was loud; dancing was taking over. A woman in the crowd held her arms high, shaking them in time with the beat.

Rachel, dancing, had always put her head down and tucked herself over and whirled her arms like threshers.

"Sarah!" he called into the mass of people, because he thought he saw her, jumping up and down in the crowd. But it wasn't her.

Then he glimpsed, in a far corner of the room, what looked like a green shirt. It was William, talking to Sarah and Fletcher. Jonathan saw her look his way; she gave him a weak smile and a little wave, and then Fletcher and William turned and saw him.

"Jonathan," William called out.

"Jonathan," Fletcher said.

"Hey, guys," Jonathan said, and came forward to join them. "I was just looking for you all."

"We've been wondering where you were," William said.

Jonathan explained, "I went in search of cigarettes. Well, Deborah and I went in search of cigarettes."

Sarah spoke in a harsh voice. "Did you have any luck?"

"Not a bit," he said to her.

"I'm surprised," she said.

"Apparently no one smokes anymore," he said.

She said, "Lots of people smoke."

"I guess I've been looking in the wrong places," he told her, and she said, "That sounds right."

William finally broke in. "We were just talking about how much we hate these kinds of parties."

"Who's ready to dance?" Sarah said.

"Let's go," William said, and she and he went off together toward the center of the room.

"Do you want a cigarette?" Fletcher asked, taking a pack from his jacket pocket.

"Good God, thank you," Jonathan said.

It seemed they were going to be friends for the night.

Jonathan said, "Let's go to the terrace."

When they got outside, they found Deborah and Kathy.

"Forgive me for running off like that," Jonathan said to Deborah.

She asked, "Did I scare you?"

"A little," he said, and laughed, and she laughed, too.

It wasn't long before Sarah and William appeared, sweaty from dancing. Jonathan took the joint from his shirt pocket and asked, "Does anyone want this?"

Fletcher held the lighter. Jonathan inhaled and then passed the joint to William, who took a puff and gave it to Kathy, who handed it to Sarah. She gave the joint to Deborah, and Deborah took a big hit before offering it to Fletcher, who had some and gave it back to Jonathan, who passed it around again.

"Are you stoned?" a voice asked. It was Sarah.

His body felt heavy, and he could clearly hear the traffic coming and going on the streets and avenues below.

"Kind of. Are you?"

"I'm on the way," she said.

William said, "I'm ready to dance some more."

"I'll go with you," Deborah said, and Kathy added, "Let's all go."

Inside, Deborah and Kathy cleared a space and began gyrating. William followed, and then Sarah, too, began to move.

Jonathan watched her sway to the left then to the right, her arms seeming to float in the air beside her; she looked as if she were in a pleasant trance, like a charmed cobra. Watching her, he felt—what? Appreciation? Affection? Love? He felt himself lucky to be with her, for she made him feel calm, and now he slid up next to her, got his arms partway around her, and lightly pulled her toward him, so that their faces came close to touching. She shut her eyes and let his hands around her waist balance her.

"You can be a jerk sometimes," she whispered to him.

"I apologize."

"I'm sick of hearing about Rachel," she said.

"I won't mention her again," he said.

"You hurt my feelings," she said, and separated herself from him and joined the other three.

He stood next to Fletcher. Without a word, they turned around and headed to the bar.

"Will that be a Scotch and soda?" the bartender asked Jonathan.

"Thanks," Jonathan said.

It was late now, almost midnight. He'd drunk too much. Had he been at the party with Rachel, she would have said, "Enough is enough," and they would have left by now.

But Rachel was gone, for good, it seemed to him at that

moment, and—it was both crushing and a relief to feel this—he was free. And though he knew that this sense of freedom from her would not entirely last, that the memory of her would overtake him again, the feeling was nonetheless substantial: He was with Sarah.

"Excuse me, do you have any cherries?" he said to the bartender.

The bartender leaned over, opened a small refrigerator, and pulled out a jar of bright-red maraschino cherries. "We're closing up," he said. "Why don't you just take the bottle."

He turned around and began opening cardboard boxes for the empty and near-empty bottles lined up on the bar.

Jonathan dug two fingers into the jar and began trying to capture the cherry with the longest stem. He pulled up one, then another, and finally found one that seemed right. He ate the cherry but kept the stem.

"Fletcher, will you excuse me?"

He stumbled away from the bar and began weaving among people.

Where were they—where were *his* people? There they were. They were still in their circle of sorts. He crossed the floor to Sarah.

"Hello," he said in her ear.

"Hello," she said.

He got down on one knee before her and took hold of her hand. Awkwardly, he curled the cherry stem around her ring finger. He made a number of tries at tying it there, but, sadly, it wasn't long enough after all, so he held it in place with his hand, clutching hers.

"What in the world are you doing?" she asked.

It was a good question—what *was* he doing? "What does it look like?" he said, and he wondered, briefly, whether he meant it, whether he would still feel this strongly about her after he'd sobered up. And he thought that he would. Surely, he would. He had the idea that he was seeing into his future, and he felt, quite naturally, at that drunken hour, that they would share it.

"Are you proposing?" Sarah asked.

He said, "I'm not sure that I can propose without a real ring. But at least you'll know."

"I'll know what?"

But he was afraid to say.

He stood and kissed her on the cheek. Then he gave her a kiss on the lips. They came closer and wrapped their arms around each other.

The party was ending. The loft's wall sconces came up brightly, and the music went down low, and in the harsher light he could see a line of people heading for the door to the elevator.

They stood together holding hands. Their new friends were with them. Everybody said what a nice time it had been, then exchanged phone numbers and promised to be in touch.

On the sidewalk in front of the building, beneath the awning, he asked Sarah, "Do you want to walk?"

Her apartment wasn't far.

"Let's walk," she said. They went toward Broadway.

Out on the avenue, the air was hotter and more humid than it had been on the terrace. A few cars and taxis drove by. He asked her which of the author's books he should read.

She said, "Everybody likes *Abel Kills Cain*, but it's not my favorite. I think you might like the new one."

They turned at the corner. There was no traffic now, and he could hear their footsteps echoing from one side of the street to the other. "I'll bring you a copy from work," she offered.

"That'd be great," he said.

He took off his jacket and slung it over his shoulder, then undid the buttons on his shirt cuffs, first the left, then the right, and rolled the sleeves up to his elbows. The moon was bright and the sky was starless. Buildings rose above them. He put his arm around her shoulder.

THE EMERALD LIGHT IN THE AIR

In less than a year, he'd lost his mother, his father, and, as he'd once and sometimes still felt Julia to be, the love of his life; and during this year, or, he should say, during its suicidal aftermath, he'd twice admitted himself to the psychiatric ward at the University Hospital in Charlottesville, where, each stay, one in the fall and one the following summer, three mornings a week, Monday, Wednesday, Friday, he'd climbed onto an operating table and wept at the ceiling while doctors set the pulse, stuck electrodes to his forehead, put the oxygen meter on his finger, and then pushed a needle into his arm and instructed him, as the machines beeped and the anesthetic dripped down the pipette toward his vein, to count backward from a hundred; and now, another year later, he was on his way to the dump to throw out the drawings and paintings that Julia had made in the months when she was sneaking off to sleep with the man she finally left him to marry, along with the comic-book collection—it wasn't a collection so much as a big box stuffed with comics—that he'd kept since he was a boy. He had long ago forgotten his old comics; and then, a few days before, he'd come across them on a dusty shelf at the back of the garage, while looking for a carton of ammo.

It was a humid Saturday morning. Thunderstorms had come through in the early hours after dawn, but now the rain and wind had passed, and the sun lit the puddles on the road and the silver roofs of the farmhouses and barns that flickered into view between the trees as he steered the ancient blue Mercedes—it had been his father's, and his grandfather's before that—across the county he'd grown up in. Maybe on his way back home he'd stop at Fox Run Farm for a gallon of raw milk. Or no. He'd drink a glass or two and then, in a month, have to dig the rest out of the refrigerator and pitch it. He reminded himself to vacuum the living room and clean the downstairs toilet. His name was Billy French, and he was carrying a Browning .30-06 A-bolt hunting rifle in the trunk of the Mercedes. He wasn't a gun nut, and he didn't hunt. He was a sculptor and a middle-school art teacher. Every now and then, he liked to stop on his way home from school and shoot cans off the rotting fence posts that surrounded the un-used cow pasture where, at sixteen, in the grass and weeds, he'd lost his virginity to Mary Doan. He hadn't thought about Mary in ages, and then, recently, he'd run into her—surprise, surprise, after all these years—at a bar in the valley. He'd rec-ognized her right away—he remembered her limp—but it had taken her a couple of tries to remember his name. They'd had a laugh over that, and he'd bought her a drink, and she'd bought him one, and now she was coming across the moun-tain, she was coming that night for dinner.

He'd told her seven thirty.

Ahead on the road, a tree limb was down. He was on a small rural route, a cut between two lanes, not much used. He stopped the Mercedes, unbuckled his seat belt, and got out. A locust bough had sheared off in the wind. The bough was long and twisting, green with crooked branches and smaller, thorny stems. His tree saw and his ax were back at the house, but it might be possible to drag the bough from the tip and more or less swing the whole thing—swing wasn't the right word, maybe—over and around and off the road, enough at least for the car to pass. He reached through the leaves and grabbed a narrow stem that stuck up in the air. There were no flowers—it was late in the season for that—but the locust's seedpods had begun to sprout, and many of these were scattered across the asphalt.

He swatted a mosquito and got the branch in both hands. The wood was damp, and the end of the bough flexed and bent when he pulled. He moved down to a thicker part, planted his feet, and leaned back. After four or five difficult heave-hos, he'd opened enough clearance, he thought, to steer the car through. He was out of breath and his shirt was wet and sticky. He got in the driver's seat and eased the Mercedes onto the oncoming side of the road. The ground sloped down from the road's edge and the soil had taken on rain. As he was working his way around the branch, wheels partly on the shoulder, the car tipped to the left and then shifted further, and a piece of ground seemed to fall away underneath. It was startling: a little slide and the Mercedes plunged. Then the tires dug in, and, abruptly, a distance off the road and at a steep angle, the car settled and stopped. Billy pushed his foot against the brake. He gripped the steering wheel. When he took his hands off, he saw that he'd scraped his palms on the locust. He was bleeding.

"Shit, fuck. Shit," he said aloud.

He turned off the engine. He hadn't slept the night before. It wasn't the thunder and lightning that had kept him up—he'd been going through the artworks that Julia had left rolled in tubes or stacked against the wall in the upstairs bedroom that had been her studio. They were piled in the backseat now. The paintings, he thought, while sitting in the car perched on the berm, were not as strong as the drawings, which, though more or less precise studies for their oil counterparts, all rural Virginia scenes—trees in a field, a dying pond, a rotting house in a mountain hollow—nonetheless had about them, with their bold erasures and smudges and retraced pencil lines, the feeling of something abstract and, in comparison with the worked and reworked paintings, complexly three-dimensional. The paintings seemed to exist as strangely flat fields—they put Billy in mind of Early American naïve art—and, in looking at them and, back in the day, talking to Julia about them, he'd come to see how purposefully she distorted light and shadow. "I'm searching for something that isn't quite there," she'd once said.

He was afraid of shifting his weight and starting another slide—the car had gone four or five feet already, and the embankment fell maybe ten more. He could hear running water. Was there a creek off in the woods? He knew this country, or thought he did, but it was always surprising him, just the same.

He wiped his hands on his pants. Gently now, he ratcheted down the brake. He eased open the driver's-side door.

Anyway, her drawings and paintings—he knew better than to throw them out, but the fact of them in his house was terrible. He'd meant for some time to do something about them. At first, of course, he'd tried to get them back to her, but she'd told him—this was during one of their five or six phone conversations since her departure, two years earlier—that her old work was no longer meaningful or important to her. "I'm not doing that kind of painting anymore," she'd said. "I'm engaged with a more total realism."

"Photo-realism?" he'd asked.

"No, nothing like that."

He was standing in the kitchen in his socks and underwear, drinking bourbon and Coke—his mother's drink. Ice rattled in the glass. The floor was brown and dirty, in need of mopping.

Julia said, "Billy, you're drinking."

Oh, God, how to get out of the Mercedes safely? The hillside was steep and the grass was wet. And what if he made it, with both feet firmly on the ground, and the car slid down on top of him?

He pushed the car door open all the way and, clutching the doorframe for balance, tumbled out onto the incline. Fuck Julia. He could take her pictures and toss them into the woods right now.

He had weed in the glove compartment. Might there be a stray Ativan or two in there as well? The thing to do was slog around to the uphill side, the passenger side, reach through the window, and feel around in the glove compartment for whatever he could find. But wouldn't you know it? He got partway around the Mercedes, and the whole car seemed to shudder and tremble. Billy watched it start into another drop— it was as if the car were shaking its wheels free of the mire— and then down the grade it rumbled, through the mud and across the grass, sliding to a rest at last in a patch of milkweed at the foot of the hill.

He felt a raindrop, and another. The clouds were not in sight yet, but Billy could sense the weight of low pressure bearing down. An emerald light was in the air. The birds and other animals had gone quiet; the world was still, as it can be when bad weather is coming. He was thinking of Mary. By the time he'd managed to have sex with Mary, back in high school—she was a senior and he was a junior, and that fact alone was thrilling—she'd already had one abortion and one marriage proposal.

He half walked, half slid down the hill. The Mercedes was sitting in a gulch between the woods and the embankment. He heard running water again—the creek had to be close. He reached gently into his pocket and took out his phone. His hands were a cut-up mess. The garage he used for

the Mercedes was on the other side of Charlottesville, close to
Julia and Mark's farm, and, anyway, too far for a tow truck to
come. Could he drive back up to the road? It didn't look
to Billy as if there'd be much room to maneuver.

Daily life's frustrations, even the big ones, no longer ruled
him, not the way they had for a long time in his life. He'd
been psychotic with agitation that had grown from his grief,
and it was hard for him to remember what that had been like,
exactly: not the grief—he had plenty of that still—but the
urge to die. He'd got all but there. He'd had the Browning
loaded. He'd had it ready and at hand, a few times.

He smelled storm. He might be able to drive for a while
beside the road. The sun was high. Billy put his phone in his
pocket and got back in the Mercedes. The car seemed all
right. He drove slowly. He was in a wide but navigable trench.
It wasn't bad driving. The trench curved slowly around to the
right, and then came to a straight section that reminded
Billy of the Roman road that he and Julia had walked a length
of during that difficult vacation in Italy, the winter before
she left.

They'd gone to see the paintings and frescoes of Tiepolo.
Billy had become vocal about Tiepolo after seeing *Bacchus and
Ariadne* in Washington, and Julia had got into him, too. After
Christmas in Rome, they had taken the train north to Ven-
ice, and had spent a week walking around in the cold, searching out churches and palazzos and wandering the Gallerie
dell'Accademia, where they had both become enchanted,
though for different reasons, with *The Rape of Europa*. Julia got
excited over the distant meeting of clouds and sea in the picture's right-hand corner, while Billy fixated on the encroaching
cloud plume to the left, the spire of pink and gray—it looked
to him like a mushroom cloud—exploding upward from behind the rocky outcropping on which Zeus, transformed into
a bull, seduces the Phoenician princess Europa, dressed in

white and attended by ladies-in-waiting. The cloud threatens to wipe them all out, but Europa and her entourage seem either unconcerned or unaware. She sits enthroned on the back of Zeus. Two other bulls wait nearby. A maid tends to Europa's hair and another bathes her feet; shepherds and an African are on hand, and putti fly about and urinate from on high, and a black bird perches on a strange little cumulus cloud that has floated in over the princess's head.

There was the creek. It came out of the woods and flowed into a concrete drainpipe that tunneled under the road. A stretch near the trees looked fordable. He could angle the car just so, over and between the rocks. Once he got to the other side, though, where was he going to go? Trees pushed against the embankment, and the way was overgrown. Billy nosed the car forward anyway. He felt a curiosity. The undercarriage of the Mercedes was not high, and when the wheels dropped into the water Billy heard and felt the bumper scrape the rocks. He jerked the car, not across but up the creek—maybe he could follow it out into a field or a yard somewhere upstream. The retirement home where his parents had ended their lives was up the way he'd come that morning, not on the little lane but on the bigger road at the end of it, heading down from the hills toward town. He saw lightning in the distance, and peered through the windshield at the dark clouds now crossing the sky over Afton Mountain.

He turned on the headlights and the wipers.

In the hospital, he'd had hallucinations. He remembered looking in his bathroom mirror—it was made of metal, not glass—and seeing his face deformed. He'd known better than to believe what he saw, but, on the other hand, he hadn't known better, far from it: There it had been in front of him, his bent, misshapen skull. Now, as he drove into the forest, Billy recalled that, for a long time, the time of the locked ward and his sick brain and the torn-up suicide notes to Julia,

he'd felt the burning. He'd felt it in his temple. It was, somehow, he knew, both imaginary and real, a beckoning, an itch,
a need for a bullet. Of course he'd thought always of the
Browning, of loading it and getting into position on the
living-room floor, or maybe out back in the barn, maybe lay-
ing down a tarp first.

The barn on the hill behind his house—that was where
he made his art. When he wasn't teaching seventh graders
how to draw, he made big untidy installations that he referred
to as his trash heaps. Along with the rifle and the comics and
Julia's art, he had in the back of the Mercedes a canvas bag
with about two dozen cans that he'd saved from trips to the
shooting pasture. He was planning to include them in a piece.
He needed more, but he didn't eat much canned food, and his
personal use of the materials in his work was crucial to him.

The thing about Mary was that her limp looked good. It
wasn't a very noticeable limp. One of her legs was shorter
than the other. Billy remembered her swaggering down the
hall in high school, thirty years before. Her father had been a
country doctor, the sort who got out of bed and drove into
the hills at all hours to treat people who couldn't pay or get
down the mountain to town. Mary was a year older than
Billy, but she'd let him put his hands down her pants. He'd
ridden his bike up Route 250, past the Episcopal church, to
her house. There was never anyone home but her. She'd been
provocative and graceful and unembarrassed. He remembered
her standing on her short leg, the other leg propped out at an
angle, toes touching the floor, a dancer's pose.

What he needed to do was fix up the car. It was a 1958
220S with a white roof and a gray interior, and there had been
rust on the body and the chrome and underneath, on the
chassis, for a long time. Billy wasn't a car buff, and didn't know
what this one might be worth cleaned up. People had offered
to buy it. He remembered riding in it with his grandfather,

who never drove faster than twenty-five miles per hour. His
grandfather had told stories, actually, of driving his old Ford
up creek beds, back in the thirties.

Billy urged the car up a mossy rise and over a little water-
fall. Branches scraped the roof.

After Julia left, in his worsening he'd walked and moved
as if crushed by some stronger form of gravity. The air had
pressed him down, and he could not get out from under it.
Some days, he'd curled in a ball on the floor and promised
himself that soon, soon, soon—it would be his gift to himself—
he'd walk up to the barn and lie down with the rifle.

The car was swamped. Or it wasn't, exactly, but the creek
had risen and the tires now made a wake. The Mercedes didn't
have much acceleration, and the steering felt loose. Billy pow-
ered over a high rock, or maybe a tree root—it was hard to
see—then, suddenly, precipitately, the wheels dropped in front
and the car slammed down and stopped.

Billy pressed the gas. The motor raced and the car shook
but didn't move. He gave the engine gas again, and the rear
wheels spun, churning the creek and throwing mud. He put
the lever in park. Lightning hit, close and loud. Billy reached
across the seat, opened the glove compartment, and felt around
for the pot. There was the registration paperwork, and there
was a pill bottle, his Ativan; and there were his pliers (he'd
recently begun preparing the cans, tearing and disfiguring
them before shooting), and the joint and the lighter, and the
driving gloves that his grandfather had worn and that Billy's
father had kept in the car after Billy's grandfather died, and
that Billy had left there after his own father died. He took the
gloves out and felt how old they were, then worked his hands
into them.

On or off—he wasn't sure what felt better.

He put the pills in his shirt pocket, turned off the igni-
tion and the wipers and the lights. He remembered how the

misery had bowed him over: He'd gone everywhere, in those days, with his head down, barreling rigidly forward, compounding the pain by moving at all; but when he touched himself to find where the pain was coming from he couldn't find the spot.

It was dark in the woods without the headlights. He lit the joint and the car glowed inside. Julia's paintings were in back. She worked with tiny brushes, and he'd wondered, sometimes, when he saw her at it, what she was thinking while she slowly built up the paint on the canvas. He exhaled smoke and watched the saplings at the edge of the creek bend in the surge.

She'd talked to him, as they stood together at the Accademia, gazing at *The Rape of Europa*, about the singular cloud hovering over Europa, its complete non-relation to the more natural-seeming clouds that dominate the painting as a whole, the delicate, pale clouds on the horizon, the spire of darker cloud rising up behind the rocks. "Everything is off in Tiepolo," she'd said. "Spatial relations don't cohere. It isn't simply that people fly with angels through the air. What world are we looking at? The paintings at all points lead the eye toward infinity." She might have been anticipating his own predicament, his own crisis of perception, when, nine months later, and again the following year, he'd lain on the operating table, crying and holding the nurse's hand, while the doctors got him ready. The hospital ceiling was white foam tile with fluorescent lights, and the doctors had looked to Billy as if they were levitating beneath them, beneath the lights—as if they, the doctors, had descended from heaven to perform electro-convulsive therapy.

Someone was coming toward the car. A figure moved between the trees beside the creek. It was a boy carrying an umbrella. He was skinny and wore jeans and no shirt. He stepped down to the bank and splashed across to the car with the umbrella over his head. Billy rolled down the window, and the rain swept in, drenching him.

"Are you the doctor?" the boy said.

"Doctor?" Billy said.

"Luther said he saw car lights. We prayed you'd come. Are you smoking pot?"

"I'm stuck on this rock," Billy said.

"I see that," the boy said.

"I was making good progress, and the next thing I knew the wheels were spinning."

"Creeks aren't the best for driving in a storm," the boy said.

Billy rolled up the car window. He opened the door and put out his foot. The rock was massive and slick; the creek was about to overtake it. He eased himself out and stood clear of the car. He was still wearing his grandfather's driving gloves and holding the joint. He lowered one foot into the creek, leaped in, and lunged toward the bank, where his feet sank into the wet earth. "I'm fine," he said. "I made it."

"Don't you have your doctor's bag?" the boy asked.

He looked to be twelve or thirteen, the age of Billy's students, but Billy didn't recognize him.

"It's our mother," the boy said.

"Your mother?"

"She's up that way." He held the umbrella over Billy, who said, "What's wrong with her?"

"It's cancer."

"I'm sorry," Billy said.

"She's up here," the boy said.

There was no need to lock the car or take the key. Billy put the joint in his shirt pocket with the pills—it would get soaked; he should have left it in the car, but there was nothing he could do about that now—and said, "I doubt I'll be able to help her. I want you to know that," and then followed anyway, a few steps behind the boy, to the place where the boy had crossed the creek on his way down. Billy watched the boy wade through the water, and then slogged in after him. The creek here was deep and fast. The car would be all right or not. Billy leaned against the torrent and struggled up onto the bank, and then he and the boy pushed ahead, slipping in the mud and on the mossy ground, pushing branches away from their faces. Once, Billy stumbled, and the boy held the umbrella over him while he got up. The umbrella was torn and bent, and water poured down it onto Billy's neck.

They went over a rise, and then walked down along what looked like a lane—maybe the land had been cleared at one time—a grassy, open promenade between the trees. The lane led into a hollow. There was a cabin, a shed, really, with a sinking roof and small square windows and a chimney over-taken by ivy. The cabin featured a porch, though not much was left of that, only a few boards elevated on piled stones, with no steps leading up from the yard to the door. The cabin had two front doors, oddly—one beside the other. Billy didn't see an actual road, or a car parked nearby, but there was trash littering the ground.

The boy hopped onto the porch, closed and shook the umbrella, and stomped clay from his shoes. Billy climbed onto the porch—he had to heave himself up—and kicked the red mud off his own heels. The boy pushed open the door on the left. "I brought the doctor," he called inside.

"Show him in," a man answered.

The boy held the door. Billy had to duck under the frame. Water ran from every part of him. The floor inside was missing in places, and the air felt cold, like a draft from underground. It smelled like the earth. Water dripped through the roof. Two windows, one in the rear and one on the side of the cabin, let in faint light—their panes, if they'd ever had any, were gone.

Billy's eyes were adjusting. The cabin seemed bigger from

inside than from out. As he came in, he saw, to the left of the door, a tumble of bags and suitcases. A dividing wall ran down the middle of the cabin, splitting the space—that explained the two front doors—and there was an interior door, partway down the dividing wall, leading to the cabin's right-hand side. The room on the left, the one he was in, might have been ten feet wide by thirteen or fourteen feet deep. The fireplace and the chimney were over in the other half.

Billy saw a bed pushed up under the window at the back of the cabin. A woman was lying in it, and a man stood over her. The man spoke to the boy on the porch: "Caleb, put down that umbrella and get the doctor something to dry himself."

Billy heard the other front door open and close, and he heard the sounds of the boy moving behind the dividing wall. Billy could feel his footfalls traveling through the floorboards.

"She's struggling," the man said to Billy.

The bed was an old iron thing with a mattress on top. The woman had a coat draped over her and a bundle of clothes for a pillow. Rain spattered the windowsill above the bed but didn't seem to be getting on her.

"We've moved her from corner to corner all night, except where the floor's out. The water follows her," the man explained.

"It's been quite the storm," Billy said.

He picked his way across the damaged floor to the bedside. His shoes squished.

"Don't fall through," the man said.

The man was bald and hadn't shaved—he wore the shadow of a beard. It was hard to tell if he was old, or maybe just Billy's age, and he spoke with an accent that reminded Billy of the Appalachian mountain speech he'd heard when he was a boy, but which, even so, he couldn't place—it wasn't local.

"I'll be careful," Billy said. He felt as if he were seeing through a fog. The splashing rain on the windowsill made a mist in the air, but it was also the pot, deranging his balance, his sense of perspective.

At the bedside, Billy leaned down and saw the woman shudder beneath the coat that was covering her. Then she was still. The door in the dividing wall opened, and the boy appeared and handed him a damp, dirty piece of cloth, a towel, of sorts.

"Thank you," Billy said.

The man said to the boy, "Go find your brother and tell him the doctor's arrived." The boy left the room through the front door. To Billy, the man said, "We didn't mean to be staying here."

They stood over the woman on the bed. Why were there no chairs? Everything looked wrecked and rotten.

Billy went down on his knees. The man said, "I know there's nothing to be done," and knelt, too.

The woman's eyes were closed and her mouth was open. Her skin seemed stretched, and her lips were parched. The man told Billy that she'd taken neither food nor water for some time. He and Billy faced each other over her. There was a moment when Billy's heart raced. The man studied him. Billy looked down. The man said, "You're not a doctor, are you?"

"No, I'm not. I'm sorry."

"But you're here."

Billy explained, "I teach junior high over in Crozet. I was on my way to the dump to throw some things out."

"The dump's not up here."

"The road was blocked. I took the creek and wrecked on the rocks."

Billy heard footsteps on the porch. The door opened and the cabin shook as Caleb and his brother came in. The brother was bigger than Caleb, older, and wore a dark shirt. They stood dripping side by side at the foot of the bed, and Billy remembered sitting at his own mother's deathbed, feeding her a mixture of morphine drops and Ativan, squeezing her hand, and telling her he would miss her, while her breaths came farther and farther apart.

The woman on the bed inhaled. Her dark hair was fanned out around her head.

The man told the boys, "I want you two to go down to the creek and bring the doctor's car."

"It's stuck," Caleb said.

"That's what the doctor told me," the man said, and added, "The doctor and I will stay with her."

"The flood may have washed it away," Caleb said.

"Go see. Go on."

The brothers backed away from the bed.

The man asked Billy his name, and in that moment, Billy could not say—he felt too disoriented to speak. He raised one hand and pulled the coat more neatly and more fully across the woman, tucking the collar around her neck; the tail reached almost to her feet. He saw that she was wearing socks. Her feet were tiny. He was shaking.

He tried to take a deeper breath. He felt his grandfather's gloves shrinking and tightening as they dried on his hands.

"I can help her," he said finally.

Light came dully through the window, and seemed to drip down between the beams overhead. Billy listened to the softening rain. He reached inside his shirt pocket and clumsily got hold of the pill bottle. He said, "This will help her rest."

It took him some time to open the cap. He peered down into the bottle. There was a handful of pills. He thought to take one himself, maybe more than one. But there were so few; he didn't. Instead, he asked the man, "Do you have any water?"

"Water?" the man said.

"Is there a tap?"

"No," the man said. "There's a pump out back."

Billy held the open bottle in one hand. With his other hand, he reached up to the window. He stuck his hand out to catch the rain in the bottle cap. He said to the man, "I want you to watch what I'm doing." Then he held the bottle cap over the woman's mouth. He let a drop, and another, fall.

He shook a pill from the bottle.

"Like this," he said.

He leaned over the woman. He held the pill unsteadily between his thumb and forefinger, between the raised seams at the fingertips of his glove. He tucked the pill beneath the woman's lower lip, near her cheek, and then reached up and caught more rain. "Give her water with the pill."

He shook the cap dry, then put it back on the bottle and told the man to give her four or five a day. "There should be enough here to get her through," he said.

"Thank you for your kindness," the man said.

After a moment, Billy left the bedside. He stepped across the broken floor planks and opened the front door. Thunder rolled in the far distance. He stood on the porch, in the drizzle, and tried to stop trembling.

It isn't the shock. It's the brain seizure, brought on by the shock. Atropine goes in, to keep the heart working. The anesthetic follows, and, after that, succinylcholine, which paralyzes the body. Life support is necessary. A blood-pressure cuff inflated tightly around one ankle keeps the succinylcholine out of the foot, which, when the shock is given, shows the seizure as twitching toes. The head and the heart are wired: electroencephalograph to scalp; electrocardiograph to body. A bite plate goes between the teeth, and an oxygen mask covers the face. The anesthetic has a sweet smell; the patient loses consciousness ten or fifteen seconds after it enters the blood. That done, the doctor places the paddles against

THE EMERALD LIGHT IN THE AIR   155

the forehead. Optimally, the seizure, the convulsion, should last twenty, thirty, forty seconds. Shorter or longer is less effective. There must be enough anesthetic in the blood to keep the patient unconscious but not so much that it soaks the brain and dampens the seizure. The anesthetic is short-lived, and the procedure is over in minutes. The anesthetic goes in, blackness comes, and then suddenly, as if nothing had taken place, the nurse's voice asks, "Can you tell me where you are?"

He heard a noise and saw lights. It was the Mercedes coming toward him along the avenue of trees.

He stepped down off the porch into the mud.

The boy was driving. His brother sat beside him. The boy parked in front of Billy, like a valet at a restaurant. He rolled down the window and called, "We brought the car."

"You brought the car," Billy said.

"The flood almost took it down the mountain."

"I thought it surely would have."

"We got it in time," the boy said, and Billy said, "Your mother is sleeping."

The boy got out, leaving the door open for Billy. "Come on," he said to his brother.

The hood and the roof were covered with leaves, and scratches and dents ran along the body of the car, where it had crunched onto the rock.

The boy pointed. "Drive between the trees and don't cross the creek. Follow the side of the mountain. Turn left at the train tracks. There's a busted fence. Go through it and drive across the field. There's an empty house and a pond. Go past the house to the gate. The road is on the other side."

"Okay," Billy said.

He watched the brothers climb onto the porch, kick the mud off their shoes, and go through the right-side door into the cabin.

Billy swept the leaves off the car with his hand—first the

roof, then the hood—and pulled more from under the wipers. He got in the car. The rain had about stopped. He rolled up the window, just in case. His scraped hands hurt beneath the gloves, but he could hold the wheel.

He drove out of the hollow, and the gray sky opened to view. He heard the rushing creek on his left, and kept going. It wasn't long before he had to thread between trees and under branches. He saw only glimpses of sky. A deer jumped in front of the car and scared him, and several times he had to back up and redirect the Mercedes around fallen logs. He didn't know how far he'd come, but he could feel the slope of the mountain rising beside him on his right.

He was on the tracks before he saw them. They were ancient and broken, buried in the weeds. He turned left and followed them. The Mercedes bumped along over the crooked ties. After a mile or so, he saw the field and the fence that the boy had told him to look for, and, beyond the field, the empty house and the pond.

He relaxed his grip on the wheel. He took his time crossing the waterlogged grass. He stopped at the gate, put the lever in park, and got out. The gate was chained and locked. He yanked on the lock. "Fuck me," he said, and walked back to the car.

He opened the trunk and retrieved the Browning, unzipped the case, and removed the rifle. He took a bullet from the box and loaded the gun. He walked over and stood about ten feet from the gate, raised the rifle to his shoulder, and aimed. It took one shot. The lock jumped and settled. Billy expelled the shell, walked up to the gate, removed the shattered lock from the chain, unwrapped the chain from the fence, and pushed open the gate. He carried the gun, the chain, and the lock to the car. He put the Browning into its case, and the lock and the chain into the canvas bag full of cans. Before shutting the trunk, he walked back to where he'd fired the gun. It took him a minute to find the shell. He picked it out of the grass, then tossed it into the bag with the other things. Before closing the trunk, he opened his box of comic books. He didn't take any out. He knew what they were, pretty much. He should have given them to the boys. He closed the trunk, took his phone from his pocket, got into the driver's seat, pulled off one of his gloves, and dialed 911. The operator, a woman, said, "What is your emergency?"

"I want to report a dying woman, a woman who's dying," he said.

"Can you tell me your name, sir?"

"My name is Billy French."

"Where are you located?"

Billy looked about. He said, "I thought I was below Afton Mountain, but things don't look right. I'm in a field. There's a vacant house near a pond."

"Can you be more specific, sir?"

Billy said, "She's in a cabin on the mountain. There's a man and two boys. You go through a field and along some rusted tracks. There's a kind of lane or alley or something in the woods."

"I'll need an address, sir."

"There is no address."

"I need to know where the woman is, sir," the operator said.

"I don't know," he said.

"Sir?"

"I'm not sure."

He hung up.

He turned off the phone and put it in the glove compartment. He put the driving glove back on his hand. He buckled his seat belt, steered up to the road, and looked both ways.

It was too late to make the trip to the dump. Mary was coming, and he had to get ready. He'd thought of braising a rabbit. Did he still have time for that?

Left or right? He turned the car to the left.

As he drove, he decided that he would keep Julia's paint-ings a while longer. He could clear some space in the attic, or stow them under a tarp in the barn.

He went over and down a hill. He had the mountains on one side and a cow pasture on the other. The sky above the mountains glowed. Soon the sun would come out and the day would be blue again. He was certain that the road would lead him somewhere familiar if he drove long enough. He rolled down the window and felt the fresh air on his face. The damp, shining road curved over the foothills, and the trees alongside seemed to become greener and lusher in the grow-ing light, and before long a car passed him going the other direction; and, a little farther down the road, he did in fact come upon a house that he recognized. He slowed the car and pulled into the driveway. How had he got so far from home? He was all the way up past White Hall.

Soft white clouds and a few birds were in the air. The thunder and lightning were over at last.

Billy circled the drive, eased the Mercedes to the road, checked both directions, and went back the way he'd come.

Keep in touch with
Granta Books:

Visit grantabooks.com to discover more.

GRANTA

Also by Donald Antrim and available from Granta Books
www.grantabooks.com

ELECT MR ROBINSON
FOR A BETTER WORLD

With an introduction by Jeffrey Eugenides

'A strange and marvellous book . . . It is a work of the utmost
originality and artistic courage and it gets better, and deeper,
each time you read it' Jeffrey Eugenides

Having accidentally inspired the local suburbanites to draw
and quarter the town's bloodthirsty mayor, Pete Robinson –
civic-minded schoolteacher and enthusiastic historian of the
Medieval Inquisition – embarks on a tenuous election campaign.
But his sleepy town has entered a period of crisis: the local park
is littered with landmines, the neighbours are building deadly
moats around their homes, and his beautiful wife, Meredith, has
discovered dark powers within herself, which threaten to
transfigure their once serene lives forever. In amongst this chaos,
can Mr Robinson satisfy the terrible will of the people?

By turns funny and phantasmagorical, fiercely intelligent
and imaginative, Donald Antrim's first novel of suburban
society turned macabre is a new American classic.

'A glorious piece of gallows humour . . . A mordant, morbid
suburban gothic rendered with a flawlessly controlled irony
that's black as midnight and dry as bone' Patrick McGrath

'A dark suburban fantasy . . . richly funny and
bizarrely familiar' *New Yorker*

Also by Donald Antrim and available from Granta Books
www.grantabooks.com

THE HUNDRED BROTHERS

With an introduction by Jonathan Franzen

'*The Hundred Brothers* is possibly the strangest
novel ever published by an American . . .[It] is also the
most representative of novels. It speaks like none of us
for all of us' Jonathan Franzen

Ninety-nine brothers (one couldn't make it) gather in their
decaying ancestral mansion. There's Rob, Bob, Tom, Paul,
Ralph, and Noah; Nick, Dennis, Bertram, Russell, and Virgil.
The doctor, the documentary filmmaker, and the sculptor in
burning steel; the eldest, the youngest, and the celebrated
'perfect' brother, Benedict. Bound by blood and a common
streak of insanity, they have come together to feast, carouse,
abuse each other, and to seek out and inter the long-lost
remains of their domineering father.

Executed with the invention and intelligence of Barthelme
and Pynchon, Antrim's taxonomy of male specimens is in
equal proportions disturbing and absurdly hilarious.

'Elegant, outrageously imagined, comic . . .
Antrim exaggerates his narrator into hilarious existence'
New Yorker

'A fiercely intelligent writer . . . This is a bravura nightmare'
New York Times